DISTANT RELATIONS

DISTANT RELATIONS

by

Peter Macey

London

DENNIS DOBSON

First published in Great Britain in 1975
by Dobson Books Ltd, 80 Kensington Church Street,
London, W8
Printed in Great Britain by Weatherby Woolnough,
Wellingborough, Northants, NN8 4BX

ISBN 0 234 77355 3

To B.

Chapter one

THE JOULE-GAUGE was on the empty mark as the little car struggled to the top of Gorse Hill and for a minute I thought I wasn't going to make it. I always used the pedals on the flat – with power at fifteen pence a megajoule who didn't – but Gorse Hill was one in ten most of the way, so it was the motor or nothing. The recharge-warning light glowed urgently as I turned on to the small square of tarmac beside the triangulation point but I was there now, and I could put it all back on the way down.

It wasn't the best view-point because it was too far away to see any details. The other watchers were mainly in the covered stands built specially on either side of the glen, but I had wanted to be alone; I wasn't sure how I was going to react at the last moment. Most people would be watching from home of course; they didn't go out as much as they had in the nineteen-eighties but that was the effect of all the cheap Brazilian stereo-vision sets flooding on the market I suppose. I switched on the little two-inch flattie on my wrist and the grinning face of Brian Howland appeared.

'Well it's still zero minus twenty-five minutes, folks, and the way I hear it's all systems go, go, go.'

It was all right for him to be cheerful. He wasn't personally involved was he?

Even on the ground from two miles away the great pillar of gleaming metal seemed to form a bridge between earth and sky. The top, a few feet below the gantry which supported it, glistened in the light of the rising sun, whose rays had still not penetrated the gloom of the valley. I turned the lens of Richard's new image-intensifier towards it but there was no discernible trace of human activity.

'I guess those two intrepid astronauts are fastening their

1

seat-belts right now,' observed the fatuous Mr Howland, 'and settling down for that long long trip to Jupiter.'

I wondered whether he really thought that was where they were going and, for that matter, whether he was really under the impression that that six-hundred foot projectile could be manned by a crew of only two. He probably was, because in all the news coverage of the last thirty years there had never been any suggestion that the mission might be a more ambitious one than that.

'And in just three months' time America's Bud Rickenfall and England's Reg Baker will be gazing down on the surface of the Solar System's largest planet, the first men ever to visit that giant mysterious world. But now folks I have to leave you for a short ad session. I'll be with you in about fifteen minutes, just in time for that thrilling moment of the actual lift-off.'

I switched off. I could do without another description of how the intrepid astronauts liked Kenny's Crunchy Pop Flakes for breakfast, had Zero-Kal Sweetener in their coffee, and wore Blindo psychedelic disposable shirts. It was all lies. They had sugar in their coffee, they hated pop flakes, and they wore old-fashioned terenylon shirts. I should know that: I'd been washing Richard's since he changed out of rompers.

For that matter there wasn't a Bud or a Reg among the lot of them. There was a John, a Peter, a Roger, Leslie, David, and there was Richard of course, the youngest of all. There was Alice, Rose, Molly, Edna, Joan, I could reel off all sixty – well fifty-nine now. Was that a matter for joy or tears? It would be a great comfort to have Sally still at Bannockside but seeing again the look on her face when she knew that the accident would make her miss the launch I could feel no satisfaction even in that.

Why did they have to go? It wouldn't help Earth's population problem. That was as good as solved now that the new birth-licence laws had received international acceptance.

'We have to go to Eden because it is there, Helen,' Richard had said. He always called me Helen. I used to wish he would call me Mother but he once told me that the Director had said he mustn't, and I suppose it wouldn't have been right really.

They had to go because it was there, just what people used to say about Everest, and that had claimed enough lives before the rail-car track was built. But what an ironical choice of names, Eden, for a planet fifteen light years from the Earth, with so little known about whether conditions would be suitable even for human survival. They said it had got oxygen in the atmosphere, and water-vapour, and the temperature was about 20°, but there was a lot more to supporting life than that, wasn't there?

'If you can't even see Eden with a telescope how do you know it is there?' I had asked.

Richard had told me. 'It shows up on the computer-enhanced multiple-scan pictures, Helen. All the planets of the nearer stars do and out of the ones that have been examined Eden is the most like Earth. So we've got to go and have a closer look at it, haven't we?'

But they must be counting down around ten minutes by now. I lifted the front of the car, stepped out into the sharp morning air, and walked over to the old concrete instrument base. Being at the highest point I was nearer to the stars, nearer than Richard, but he would be passing me soon. There was still nothing to see in the valley, and I switched on my video disc again.

'Well folks this is your own Brian Howland back again, and here at the International Jupiter Mission it's zero minus nine minutes forty-five seconds and still counting.'

Desperately I peered through the image-intensifier but I could see no sign of life. I don't know what I expected; the tall pointed tower of shining metal stood on the wide space of the launching pad looking as permanent as the Empire State Building and almost as high. A thin wisp of white vapour near the base was perhaps the only clue that within ten minutes it would have gone from the Earth. Brian Howland had noticed it too.

'Yes. There's the liquid oxygen pumped in, ready for the

stage-one ignition. Now isn't it a sobering thought that here in the year two thousand and five we're still using chemical fuel to lift off our rockets? Young Bud and Reg are sure going to be glad when they're far enough out to light the fusion motor.'

I couldn't help thinking that here in the year two thousand and five we weren't allowed to use chemical fuel to drive our cars. Wasting natural resources they said, but how much natural resources were they wasting to blast off that gigantic contraption?

Brian Howland chattered on, but I wasn't really listening. Now there was someone else being interviewed; wasn't it Hank Bonding, the leader of the first Mars expedition?

'Yes Brian I sure envy those two lucky guys in the driving seat of that little chariot there.'

Hank Bonding was the vice-president of North American Space Inc., so he must have known a great thing like that couldn't be driven by a crew of two. But then perhaps it was a matter of how you looked at it. Perhaps there were only two people there waiting to ride out to the stars on a column of radioactive fire. Perhaps there were only two, but they weren't called anything like Bud Rickenfall and Reg Baker.

Brian Howland was talking again. 'Yes folks this is really it now. Ten, nine, eight, seven, six, five, four, three, two, one, zero. Yes. We have ignition. There she goes.'

The base of the rocket was hidden by dense smoke through which the fierce red combustion glowed. For seconds the huge ship remained as if anchored to the ground, as if gravity would prove too strong for it after all, but incredibly slowly it began to rise, and then suddenly it had gone. I turned the image-intensifier upwards and saw the thin black rectangle with a tail of fire.

'So long Bud. Goodbye Reg. Bon voyage and happy landings,' said the commentator.

'Goodbye Alan. Goodbye Don. Goodbye Bob, Stan, and Tom. Goodbye Mary and Betty,' I said. 'Goodbye to all of you, and especially goodbye Richard.'

I could see every one of them. I could remember them sitting at their desks, and at assembly. Right from the start I had known every one by name. They'd been very careful to give them all different names, and there was another thing, do you know there weren't two with exactly the same colour hair or eyes?

Sadly I got back in the car, using the last drop of power to drive out on the slope. It was nice to think that the battery would be charged up again when I reached the bottom.

Sally would be waiting at the cottage. Poor Sally. She was just about the same age as I had been on that autumn day in 1975 when Andrew and I had come to Bannockside, bursting with enthusiasm for the bright future which Andrew's new job held out. Now it was two thousand and five and tomorrow I must go to the Memory Deletion Centre to forget everything about it.

Chapter two

AT SCHOOL in Dartford and then at teachers' training college I had always hated the name of Helen.

'The face that launched a thousand ships,' they would say. 'Well yours wouldn't launch a rowing-boat would it?' Of course they couldn't foresee the future any more than I could.

Perhaps I should have been different if I'd gone to a mixed school; probably not though. I expect it was just the way I was made because all the other girls seemed to have plenty of boy-friends; two of them had living proof, and neither of them was sure who was the father. At least I escaped that embarrassment.

My parents had both been killed before I started school and I was brought up by an unmarried aunt. Aunt Ada died during the last term before I left college and then I was completely on my own.

It wasn't too bad during my first year's teaching because it seemed to take up all my spare time preparing lessons, but in the second year I found my leisure time hung very heavily. I used to look round museums, and there were plenty to go to, as well as Madam Tussaud's, the Planetarium, Westminster Abbey, St Paul's Cathedral, and the Tower, but eventually there comes a time when you feel you've seen it all. Of course they'd all have been ten times more interesting if I'd had someone to go with.

'What you need, you know, is a bit of torrid passion,' said Josie Bernstein, who had started teaching at the Bridge Road Infants' School the year before I had, and who shared a flat with me.

'Such as Mr Bradishaw?' I suggested.

The aging Romeo in charge of Form IVa hopefully offered his torrid passion to every young woman within sight. In one moment of desperate loneliness I had seriously considered his invitation to dinner at the Royal Hotel, but I knew what he would expect in return, and the thought of his soft clammy hands touching my body disgusted me.

'Of course not, silly. You want someone like my Les, only don't go getting ideas about him because I'll scratch your eyes out.'

'I don't think I'm quite Les's type,' I sighed. 'I'm sure he likes girls with a bit more life in them.'

'You only just need the right man to get you going you know,' said Josie. 'I've seen those quiet mousey types like you before.'

'Thank you very much.'

'No. I'm sorry. I didn't mean it like that. I mean if you could just find the right man to turn you on there'd be no stopping you.'

'Where do I find him?'

'You've got to decide what you're looking for first. Exactly what type do you fancy?'

I did know what he was like. A picture of him formed in my mind each night as I lay waiting for sleep. He held me in his arms and stroked my brow. Sometimes he kissed me, and sometimes he did more. I knew exactly what he was like, everything, even his name.

'You must know what type you fancy,' Josie insisted.

'He's quite tall, with dark hair, not too long. He's rather quiet, with a sense of humour, and he's very thoughtful. You couldn't say he's good-looking but he's got laughing eyes, and his name's Andrew.'

'You have got someone then. You certainly are a deep one. I never guessed. Congratulations.'

'It's just a dream, just someone I imagined, someone I made up.'

'I'm sorry. But never mind. At least we know what we're looking for. Now I wonder where we can find him. There's only three men under thirty on the staff here, and two of them are married. That leaves Albert Weddell.'

'Mr Blackboard Jungle himself. No, I don't think he's Andrew.'

7

'We shall have to look further afield then. Do you know anything else about this dream man?'

'He's about twenty-five, quite slim and he's very clever. I think he's some sort of a scientist.'

'If you're going to be as particular as that you'll have to use the computer-dating.'

'You mean a matrimonial agency? I couldn't do that.' Looking back it seems difficult to believe that I should have been shocked at such an ordinary and sensible thing, but in those days hardly anyone went to a matrimonial agency and the use of a computer was considered a very way-out gimmick. Nowadays, of course, even people who meet casually would naturally have a routine compatability check before they got married. Josie must have been ahead of her time.

'The way I see it Nellie, if you're going to be as specific as that it's going to take a computer to sort out your requirements. And don't forget we've got to find someone that fancies you. You might not be everyone's cup of tea.'

'Thank you very much,' I said again. It is nice to have frank and honest friends, isn't it?

*   *   *

Back in 1975, if you remember, electronic computers were very primitive, and they always seemed to work pitifully slowly. They could do so many thousand calculations a minute, but it always took about three weeks to get an answer to even the simplest question. Andrew used to say it was something to do with communication between man and computer. I mean the real Andrew, of course, not the imaginary one I told Josie about.

Anyway, with a lot of pushing from Josie I filled in an incredibly complicated form from the computer-dating matrimonial agency, and sent it off with two copies of the best photo I could find. I couldn't help thinking as I put them in the envelope that Josie was right; I wasn't everybody's cup of tea. So I wasn't surprised that nothing much came of it, nothing except a postcard acknowledging my communication and assuring me that it would be processed with the utmost despatch. After six weeks Josie suggested I should write and ask for my money back, but then two weeks later I had the letter.

'Dear Miss Rank,' it said, 'I have been given your name and address by Digital Dating Inc. and I should like to meet you. I am a U.S. citizen, aged 26, weight 156 pounds, and I am just finishing a post-doc fellowship in metallurgy at Aberdeen University. You can see what I look like from the enclosed photograph, and if you are willing to meet me I will be at St Pancras Station at 8-00 hours next Saturday, assuming the train arrives on schedule. Yours sincerely, Ebenezer Garth.'

'This had better be one of those whirlwind romances,' commented Josie, 'otherwise it's going to cost someone a fortune in train fares.'

'It might have helped,' I said, 'if we had asked the computer to find someone who didn't live too far away. They could surely have found a better specimen than that without going further north than Swiss Cottage.'

'He's probably got hidden depths,' suggested Josie, 'and perhaps the picture doesn't do him justice. Anyway you'd better look him over now you've got so far.'

*   *   *

I wanted to get a look at my date before he saw me so I sat on a seat near the platform exit and hid behind a newspaper. The face in the photograph was so nondescript that I was worried whether I should recognize him, but I needn't have bothered. The first passenger off the overnight train from Scotland was a tall lean figure in a grey raincoat, carrying a canvas zip-bag and wearing a large badge made from a disc of white card bearing the words, 'Ebenezer Garth, Aberdeen'. He stood by my seat looking utterly lost.

'Good morning Ebenezer. Did you have a comfortable journey?'

'Why Helen. It's good to see you. I was worried I might

9

not recognize you. I've got a terrible memory for faces and your picture was a bit ... '

'Nondescript?' I suggested.

'No,' he protested with embarrassment. 'Your face was in the shadow.'

'Come and have a cup of tea. Have you had any breakfast? Let's go in the station buffet.'

I got two large cups of tea and put them on the table between us. We looked at one another until the silence became embarrassing. I tried to think of something to say.

'Ebenezer is an unusual name, isn't it?'

'There were a few back in Colorado Springs, but you can call me Eb if you like.'

'Lucky my name isn't Florence.'

'Florence? Why?'

'We'd be Eb and Flo, see?'

He laughed politely, but I wasn't sure whether he thought it was funny or not. And I'd specially put on the form that I wanted someone with a sense of humour too.

'You aren't drinking your tea, Eb.'

He took a sip, then screwed his face up in displeasure.

'British Railways tea,' I apologized. 'I'll make you a proper cup later on.'

'No it's not that Helen. I don't usually drink tea. I don't like it.'

'I'm sorry. I should have asked. I'll get you some coffee.'

I snatched his cup and rushed to the counter.

'There,' I said, putting the fresh cup in front of him. 'British Railways coffee.'

He sipped it appreciatively and a thought crossed my mind.

'You know Eb that could be a good omen.'

'A good omen? Why?'

'My friend Josie says I'm not everybody's cup of tea.'

He laughed again but I'm sure he didn't think it was funny. 'That's a very interesting example of a British metaphor without a U.S. counterpart.'

After a breakfast of three doughnuts and two more cups of coffee, Eb informed me, 'I've booked for the night in a hotel in Notting Hill. Is that far from here?'

'About three miles I should think, but you don't need to check in until tonight do you? Where would you like to go now?'

'I don't know. Where is there near here?'

'The British Museum is just across the Euston Road,' I said diffidently, ashamed of my lack of inspiration.

'The British Museum. Say, that sounds real interesting. Let's go there. What time do they open?'

We spent all the morning looking round the museum. For me it was the fifth time and I thought it might have been more fun to be with someone else, but it wasn't. Eb was interested in all the things I wasn't, and every time he looked at anything he made notes about it in a little black book; I can't imagine what for.

'Wal that sure is mighty interesting, Flo.'

'My name is Helen, Eb.'

'Sorry Hel.'

'Helen, Eb.' Maybe it was me that didn't have the sense of humour and I don't think he was actually trying to irritate me but he was certainly succeeding.

We had a rather unappetizing lunch in an expensive but not very clean café somewhere around the Tottenham Court Road, and then we discussed how to spend the afternoon.

'Don't you have some place called the "Science Museum" or the "Natural History Museum" or something? That sounds like it might be a real exciting place to pay a visit to.'

' "The Science Museum" and the "Natural History Museum" are both in South Kensington, on the other side of Hyde Park,' I told him, without enthusiasm.

'You mean they've got two museums side by side? That sure is a swell idea. We could do the two of them in one go.'

'Wouldn't you rather do something else? How about going to the pictures?'

'Suits me. That was a fine-looking picture place we saw in Leicester Square. We'll go there.'

11

'I've seen that film,' I told him. 'We'll buy a paper and see what else is on.' I was terribly self-centred in those days. Perhaps I still am. It's difficult to be sure about yourself, isn't it?

After reading all through the entertainment pages of the evening paper we came to the conclusion that the only film I wanted to see was in Canning Town, so that's where we went. I can't remember what it was called but it was the worst film I have ever seen, and that includes the ones I've seen on the amateur video channels.

Ebenezer came to the flat for dinner. Josie had cooked it, which I thought was very generous, but she said she would expect me to do the same for her if the need arose. I don't know what she meant by that because when Les came to visit Josie they didn't seem to waste time eating, although I couldn't be sure because I always used to go for a walk, unless it was raining and then I went to the pictures.

'So long you two then,' said Josie, after I had introduced Eb to her and they had chatted brightly for a few minutes. 'So long now. Everything's either in the oven or the frig. I've got to be off because Les is taking me to a new discotheque he's found.' And she slipped out of the door.

'I think your room-mate's a real swell person,' Eb informed me, and that was all he said for about the next forty minutes.

Without a word we ate Josie's delicious mushroom soup, grilled rumpsteak, and peach meringue glacé, and then my companion ventured his second remark of the evening.

'There's no doubt about it your room-mate's a mighty fine cook.'

'Unfortunately she's spoken for,' I told him. 'There's a character called Les who's six feet one, has karate lessons every Tuesday evening, and plays wing threequarter for the Barbarians.'

'I didn't mean it like that Helen.'

'It's no good though, is it Eb?'

'What do you mean?'

12

'The computer made a mistake. In thinking we were suited I mean. It was stupid anyway picking two people who live so far apart. We don't even belong to the same country.'

'Well I didn't look at it like that honey,' he said gently. 'I reckoned that if the computer picked a girl in London for a guy in Aberdeen it must have gone to a lot of trouble, and you must be the only girl in the whole of Great Britain that would do.'

For a moment I almost believed him, but he was just being gallant.

'It's no good Eb. You were disappointed as soon as you saw me. You wouldn't have come if I'd sent you a clearer photo, and I shouldn't have let you come because I knew from your picture it wouldn't be any good. I'm sorry I made you waste all that money on the train fare.'

'It wasn't wasted ma'am. It's been a pleasure to have made your acquaintance, and I've had a very interesting day in London. I think perhaps I had better see if I can find this hotel I'm booked in at though now.'

I didn't answer at first, and Eb moved towards the little cupboard where he had put his coat and bag.

'I could show you round the Tower of London in the morning, and we could go for a boat trip on the river. Even though we've decided we're not suited there's no reason why you shouldn't see a bit more of London before you go back to Scotland. Your train's not until tomorrow evening is it?'

'That's most civil of you ma'am, and I sure would be interested to see the Tower. What time would you like me to call for you?'

* * *

Dr Garth called at 9 a.m. next morning and we went straight off on our sight-seeing tour. Now that we had decided we weren't suited I felt much more relaxed and I think he was too. It didn't make him any more talkative but I enjoyed showing him all the familiar landmarks and telling him all the little bits of history I remembered. He didn't say much but he listened intently to everything I said and several times I thought he was going to take out his little black notebook and jot it all down.

We had a picnic lunch in Green Park, then the river trip to Chiswick and back, and before I had noticed the day had gone by and we were sitting in the station buffet at St Pancras again.

'Are you going back to America when you've finished your research?' I asked him.

'I don't know yet. There's a job in Scotland I've applied for. It's the people that gave me the research fellowship but I don't know whether they'll take me on permanently. It's all hush-hush at the moment but if I got it I should be domiciled in the U.K. for the duration of the project.'

'That sounds very mysterious. Anyway I hope you are successful.'

'Thank you ma'am.'

We hardly said anything else until the train came in but after I had waved goodbye to him and watched the train disappear round the bend in the line I felt terribly let down. It had been foolish to expect anything to come of the computer-dating scheme, because you couldn't treat people as if they were numbers, feed them into a machine and get the answer printed out on a piece of paper. I know people don't talk like that now, but this was 1975 remember. People still had a lot of their old irrational fear of machines; they didn't realize that it was just a matter of intelligent application, taking into account the total complexities of human emotion and so on. I knew that Josie would say I ought to write to the agency and ask them to try again, but I wasn't going to. If I were destined for a lonely life I could make the best of it.

As I came out of the station the late editions of the evening papers were on sale, and I noticed new headlines on the billboards. 'England Doomed', which presumably referred to the test match, had been replaced by 'Ross and Cromarty for Jupiter Shot' but I didn't know what it meant, and it never occurred to me that it might have any bearing on my future.

14

I didn't expect to hear any more from Ebenezer Garth but I should have realized that courtesy would oblige him to write and thank me for showing him round London. His letter was quite short and formal, and it concluded, 'By the way, I got the job I was telling you about. It is with the new "Four Power Space Agency".' I felt the least I could do was write and congratulate him.

*   *   *

I found I thought about Ebenezer more than I expected to. I wondered what his new job was like and when he was starting. I wondered what his digs were like in Aberdeen, whether he had any friends up there, and what he did in the evenings. It was a pity we hadn't been suited because he was a very kind and courteous person and I felt he needed someone to look after him. But for the last two weeks of term I concentrated my daytime thoughts on the Bridge Road Infants' School and at night I thought about Andrew. Perhaps one day I should meet him. After all Ebenezer had been quite a near miss, and really Andrew and Ebenezer had a good few things in common.

Three weeks after Ebenezer had been to London I had a letter from him inviting me to Aberdeen. 'I know we've agreed to forget about the computer-dating thing,' he wrote, 'but I just wondered whether you might let me show you Aberdeen in repayment for your kindness in showing me London. It's a beautiful city and the beach is delightful in July but if you feel that it is not worth such a long journey I shall quite understand.'

I travelled overnight that Friday.

'I really wasn't disappointed when I first saw you Helen,' Eb told me as we lay on the beach for the tenth successive day.

'But I'm so plain. I've always known I was plain and it's no good pretending any different.'

'That's the most ridiculous statement I've ever heard,' Eb insisted. 'There's no such thing as a plain woman and that's a scientifically established fact.'

'What do you mean?' I asked.

15

'You must have read about the photographer who took pictures of a hundred different women, chosen at random, enlarged them all to exactly the same size and superimposed them to get one plain average definitive woman.'

'No. What was the result?'

'Venus de Milo with arms. It's true. The nearest to a definition of female beauty you could get would be plain ordinary averageness. Everything not too big and not too little.'

'Everything?'

'Everything.'

I laughed. 'Well perhaps there is hope for me then, but how about men?'

'I don't think it's been tried on men. It would depend on what sort of picture the average woman has of her ideal man. Do you have a picture of an ideal man Helen?'

'Of course.'

'Tell me about him then.'

I told him as well as I could, but somehow the details had got blurred. I thought I had a very clear picture but there were all sorts of things I couldn't remember now. 'Anyway,' I concluded, 'he's intelligent and considerate, and he's got a wonderful sense of humour and I think his name is Andrew.'

'Andrew is it? Well I can help there. My name is Andrew.'

'You said Ebenezer.'

'Ebenezer Andrew Garth. You can look in the parish register back in Colorado Springs if you don't believe me.'

I never did get to Colorado Springs so I didn't know if he was telling the truth until four weeks later I saw his name on the marriage licence, and I couldn't be angry with him then, could I? Anyway I always called him Andrew from then on.

Ten days after the wedding we came to Bannockside.

Chapter three

WHEN WE arrived in Andrew's old car that morning in
early September I thought Bannockside was the most
beautiful place in the world. I still do, but now every
corner is filled with memories and associations. Then
everything was new and fresh, and totally different from
what I had known in London.

Andrew was terribly excited about his job with the
Four-Power Space Agency – that's what they called it at
the beginning you know, when Russia and China were in
it as well – and I shared every bit of his enthusiasm.

We drove through the village in the austere beauty of
the Scottish countryside and I wondered where it could
possibly be that Andrew was to work, but where the road
ran alongside the loch an almost concealed turning on the
right led up into the hills. As the car slowly turned into it
I saw the notice 'Ministry of Agriculture and Fisheries.
Grouse Packing Station.'

'Is that near the space station?' I asked.

'That is the space station.'

I don't think I replied to that, and there wasn't much
you could say was there?

'I told you it was all very hush-hush,' Andrew reminded
me.

'Surely the local people must know it isn't a packing
station.'

'I don't suppose it fools many of them; half of them
have been working on the construction anyway.'

The road, which had appeared so insignificant from the
loch, had now broadened out into a three-lane highway
but it didn't seem to lead anywhere, except up into the
hills. Then gradually it curved to the right and suddenly
in front of us was a flat-roofed concrete city.

'The grouse packing station,' murmured my new husband.

'But the project was only begun a few weeks ago,' I stammered. 'How did they get all that built?' I had expected to see them just about digging the foundations.

'It was only announced a few weeks ago,' Andrew explained, 'but actually it's been in full swing for about two years. The Director told me about it when I came for the interview. It was decided not to announce it until the four-power agreement was all signed and sealed, and enough work had been done to indicate that a manned flight to Jupiter was at least feasible.'

The car stopped at a sort of level-crossing barrier and a distinctly slant-eyed looking guard in an olive-green uniform approached Andrew's side.

'Good afternoon Dr Garth. The Director sends his regards and hopes you had a pleasant journey. If you will report at the main entrance the commissionaire will arrange for you to be taken to meet the Personnel Officer.'

The barrier lifted, apparently without assistance from any human agency, and the car moved forward, but suddenly the sun had stopped shining and an icy hand clutched at my throat. What terrible place had we come to? Could those forbidding buildings in front of us be only two miles from the delightful village we had just passed through?

'He was Chinese,' I gasped, as we stopped at the front-door. 'And how did he know you?'

'There will be a lot of Chinese and Russians here, and I expect the guards have photos of all the staff so they can recognize them.'

'Andrew. I don't think I'm going to like it here. I think we've made a terrible mistake. I'm frightened Andrew.'

He squeezed my hand. 'Everything's going to be all right darling. You'll find there'll be a lot of people like us here. And remember you've got me to look after you now.'

I gave his hand an answering squeeze. It was an immense comfort to have Andrew, but it wasn't myself I was frightened for. I was frightened for him.

*   *   *

It really was an enormous establishment, with labs, workshops, and offices, as well as houses for the staff, shops, and recreation facilities, everything. It wasn't nearly as frightening as I had thought on the first day and in fact the station hostel, where we stayed while our accommodation was being arranged, was like a luxury hotel. I didn't like the staff houses though. The first weekend after we arrived Andrew took me to look at one that was almost finished.

'There Helen. What do you think of that?'

'It's very modern,' I said.

'This one is booked you know, but Mr Baron says we can have the next one. That'll only be another two or three weeks.'

We looked at the wonderful labour-saving kitchen, and the beautiful pink-tiled bathroom, at the small dining-room, the larger sitting-room, and the two bedrooms both with built-in wardrobes. The garden, at present an area of bare earth, tin cans and broken bricks, was a good size and it looked out on a vista of high heather-clad moors. It was a glorious view, marred only by the fifteen foot barbed-wire fence we saw it through.

'Do you think you would be happy here, my darling?'

I didn't answer, and Andrew took me in his arms.

'You don't like it, do you Helen? What's the matter honey? Is it too small?'

'Oh Andrew. I am sorry. It's lovely really, so modern and so comfortable.'

'But you don't like it, do you? What's the matter? It's the fence, isn't it?'

'It's like Belsen Andrew. I don't want to live in a camp inside a barbed-wire entanglement.'

'It's only to keep intruders out, not to keep us in you know.'

'Why does it have to be right at the bottom of our garden?' I said. 'There will be no fairies at the bottom of our garden; they can't get through the barbed-wire.'

Andrew laughed good-humouredly. 'I'm sure they could slip through in between the strands, but the fence has to be at the end of the garden because the houses are all built round the perimeter of the station.'

'I don't think I like the idea of living in a place with a perimeter anyway, let alone one marked out in barbed wire, and I suppose just down the road there's a little nest of Chinese machine-gunners, and a Russian anti-tank battery.'

'It's not quite as bad as that, but there might be an alternative you know.'

'What do you mean?'

'A cottage in the village, say. How about that?'

'Oh Andrew. Could we? Would it be possible?'

'As a matter of fact it would. When I came for the interview I decided that living on the job might be too much of a good thing and I asked the Director about living out.'

'What did he say?'

'He didn't like the idea, but I guess I kinda made it a condition. They must have wanted me pretty . badly because he gave in without arguing any.'

I had suspected before that Andrew was not just any old metallurgist. 'Why didn't you tell me?' I asked.

'Wal honey, there are disadvantages. It's not going to be so comfortable is it? Those cottages aren't exactly fitted out with gas-fired central heating. In fact we'll probably be doing well if we find one with an inside toilet. I wanted to see what you thought about the company houses before I mentioned it.'

Poor Andrew. I flung my arms round his neck and nearly knocked him over. He didn't look as if he minded though.

'Then we will take it as agreed that we prefer a cottage in the village.' By the way I had decided that he had got a sense of humour, but it was a bit more subtle than mine.

*   *   *

There weren't many houses available in that area but

20

however many we'd had to choose from I felt that we couldn't have found a better one than 'Tidal Cottage'. Andrew suggested the name and I'm afraid he had to explain it to me.

'The sea is miles away,' I protested, 'and there's no tide in the loch.'

'I know, but "Tidal Cottage" is for Eb and Flo.'

'We aren't . . .'

'Of course, I forgot. We'll call it "Cosy Nook".'

'We jolly well won't,' I insisted, 'and we won't call it "Chez Nous", or "Mon Repos", or "Dunromin". "Tidal Cottage" will do fine.'

It was the last one of about a dozen houses strung along the road by the loch and I'd guess about a mile and a half from the Station, a few minutes for Andrew in the car and not too far if he wanted to walk.

We must have been pretty dewy-eyed in those days because it was really extremely run-down. Mrs McGregor next door said that there hadn't been anybody in it for over three years, but since we didn't pay much for it we could afford to spend a bit doing it up and we had limitless energy for the job. For a metallurgist Andrew was a remarkably good carpenter, bricklayer, plasterer, and decorator, and, to my great astonishment, plumber. I still regard plumbing as one of the deeper mysteries of life, but even central heating had no terrors for Andrew.

'I think coal will be best, don't you Helen?'

'I should think so, but you aren't going to do it are you?'

'Of course.'

'But you don't know anything about it.'

'Not at the moment. It'll take me a few weeks reading up before I can make a start I'm afraid, but the librarian is getting me a couple of the standard works from the National Lending Library.'

And that was that. Andrew completed it in four weekends and about fifteen evenings, and it's worked steadily ever since. When coal-heating was banned in the nineteen nineties I had the boiler taken out and the house

21

connected up to the local thermal grid, but I'm still using the original radiators.

*   *   *

Although Andrew's work was so highly secret he never used to mind telling me about it and, in fact, it seemed to help him to solve some of the problems. I never suggested any solutions, of course, but after Andrew had been explaining some technical difficulty in words of one syllable he would suddenly see the answer. Dr Sanders would have gone up the wall if he'd known, not that he need have worried because I hardly understood a thing of what Andrew told me. I knew that they were trying to develop a new alloy for a rocket that was apparently being sent to Jupiter, but that was about my lot. I was so naive at first that I thought the entire station was occupied furiously searching for this elusive alloy.

'No Helen. Metallurgy is only a little bit of it. It's one of the smallest departments in the place. There's Engineering, Fuel Chemistry, Electronics, Navigation, Biology ...'

'Biology? What's that got to do with rockets?'

'Actually it's a bit of a mystery. It includes Space Medicine which is fair enough because after all it's going to be a manned rocket and the crew will obviously be subjected to some pretty unusual stresses, but why should we have a whole block devoted to Cytology and Tissue Culture, and another one exclusively for Genetics?'

It just went straight over my head I'm afraid. 'Who will be going on the rocket?' I asked. 'Is it anyone we know?'

Andrew laughed. 'I'm sure they haven't been chosen yet. They may not even have been born yet. The mission isn't planned for this century you know.'

'Will it take you thirty years to find that alloy then?'

'I should hope not, but there are a helluva lot of other things to do as well.'

I think I told you about all the Russians and Chinese at the Space Station. There were a lot of Americans too, but I didn't regard them as foreigners with Andrew being one.

I asked him once why, with three big powers like Russia, China, and America, they decided to build the station in Britain.

'It was because the other three were all so suspicious of one another,' Andrew explained. 'Britain being the smallest and weakest none of them could regard her as any kind of a threat or rival.'

'How convenient for them,' I said, my national pride somewhat squashed.

But when we'd been at Bannockside for about six months the Chinese and Russians suddenly disappeared. One day they were there and the next day they'd gone, and nobody seemed to know why.

'There's been an almighty bust-up somewhere up at the top, but I don't know what it's about,' Andrew told me.

It wasn't until many years later, after Dr Sanders had retired, that I learned from the new director, Dr Franks, about the bitter controversy over the sperm and egg banks.

*   *   *

I have often tried to imagine what course events would have taken if Andrew had not volunteered for Dr Randle's tests. Would everything have turned out completely differently for us, or would something else have happened to bring us back to some predetermined life-line? Perhaps he had no choice. Perhaps volunteering was part of his destiny.

Dr Randle was Head of Space Medicine and his part in the project was to find out what special stresses the crew of the rocket would have to withstand, to determine how men would react under those conditions, and to develop ways of helping them to survive. He didn't have a regular supply of human guinea-pigs for this purpose and so he had to rely on volunteers from other departments.

'There's no need for you to volunteer, Andrew,' I told my husband. 'It's not your job. You're a metallurgist. You didn't come here to be experimented on.'

'There's really nothing to it Helen. It's just a matter of

having my blood-pressure, pulse-rate and so on measured under various conditions, and it only occupies a couple of hours about once a fortnight.'

'That's not the point. It's the principle of the thing.'

'Well the way I see it all our work is leading up to the building of this great rocket thing to take some poor blighters off to Jupiter and the least we can do is to try and make sure they get a comfortable ride.'

I didn't like it but there wasn't anything I could do, and Andrew seemed to take it all so lightly that I decided I was really worrying about nothing.

Life was very pleasant at Bannockside and Andrew enjoyed his work enormously. I know I shouldn't say it but the whole place seemed to have a less sinister aspect now the Russians and Chinese had gone. The general opinion at the station was that the communists were cooking up some fantastically ambitious project of their own and this caused a great sense of competitiveness and urgency. The enthusiasm of the staff was really quite incredible considering that they were working on something that wasn't going to happen for another twenty-five years, and incidentally I found it very difficult to understand why it should take such a long period of preparation.

Sometimes Andrew would drive up to the Space Station, but if it was a nice day he would quite often walk. During our first year there he taught me to drive and once I had taken the test I was able to use the car to explore the countryside. Andrew was usually home by six, which was just as well since he was still putting a lot of work in on doing up the cottage

Although Andrew dismissed the experiments in the Space Medicine Department so lightly I could see they took it out of him. He would be much more tired than after an ordinary day's work.

'No. We weren't doing anything strenuous, Helen my love. Just normal work, but at slightly elevated temperatures,' he explained on one occasion. 'They tried us out doing mathematical calculations under conditions of increased pressure and a hundred percent humidity,' he told me another time. Once they had him working with a high noise level, another time standing on his head in the dark.

So it wasn't surprising that those evenings Andrew used to give his D.I.Y. house improvement a miss. We would sit and watch the television, listen to a few records, or more often just talk. One evening he didn't want to talk much, he just sat staring at the carpet.

'What's the matter Andrew? Is something bothering you?'

'Just something I can't quite figure, but don't worry. I'll sort it out,' and he stared at the geometrical patterns on the carpet.

'Was it very exhausting today?'

'No it wasn't exhausting at all. They let us off very lightly – just a few psychological tests and that sort of thing, just a few questions in connexion with a personality assessment programme Paul Randle was designing.'

'What can't you understand? Couldn't you answer the questions?'

'I answered them all right, but I couldn't understand my answers.'

'That sounds double Dutch to me.'

I knew Andrew would tell me all about it, but I didn't press him. I just fetched us both another cup of coffee and some of the chocolate biscuits we used to gorge ourselves on in those days.

'It wasn't Dr Randle that was asking the questions,' Andrew went on. 'They were all on tape and there was some music that sort of hypnotized me. Paul said I mustn't be inhibited and I must answer all the questions immediately without thinking about them. He said I mustn't worry that I was committing myself to anything because it was all hypothetical, just ironing out the bugs in his personality programme.'

I put my arm round Andrew's shoulder to try and reassure him, but he almost seemed as if he didn't know I was there.

'It was a strange voice. It said, "Supposing there were a

25

star five, ten, twenty light-years from the earth, with a system of planets like the sun's. Supposing one of them were just like our world, with equable temperatures, a breathable atmosphere, with oceans and continents, mountains, plains, valleys, rivers, and vegetation. Supposing it were possible to build a space-ship to visit that planet. Would you volunteer to go on that space-ship?" And I said, "Yes of course I would." Straightaway I said it without a moment's thought or hesitation.'

Now it was my turn to be alarmed. 'What does it mean Andrew? What is going to happen?'

'Nothing is going to happen my sweet. It was just hypothetical, just trying out a new personality test.'

'But you aren't an astronaut. You didn't come here to fly in a rocket. You're a metallurgist. You work in the laboratory at the station.'

'I know Helen. I tell you it's nothing to worry about honey. I was just puzzled to know why I should volunteer for a one-way trip like that.'

'One-way trip?' I stammered.

'The time it would take to get there it would be a bit pointless coming back. They'd all have died of old-age wouldn't they?'

'Andrew. Andrew.'

'But it's all hypothetical. As you say, I'm a metallurgist not an astronaut. This rocket we're working on isn't going to be ready this century, and by the time it is I'd be too old to be a member of the crew. Anyway it's not going to a distant star, is it? It's going to Jupiter.'

Chapter four

IT WAS quite surprising really how well we settled down in Scotland. I had spent the first twenty-two years of my life in or near London and you could hardly imagine anywhere more different than Bannockside. I suppose it was strange for Andrew too, but since he had been living in Aberdeen when we met I sort of regarded him as half Scottish. I'd never really been happy in London and I only went back once in the first two years. That was for Josie's wedding. Andrew and I drove down in the car. We'd got a new one now, only a Mini, but it was a bit more reliable than the old one. We decided we'd had enough of that when the bearings disintegrated one holiday weekend halfway up the Electric Brae. Or was it halfway down?

'We finally made it you see,' said Josie, 'but you two beat us by eighteen months.'

'Not my fault,' insisted Les. 'I've been trying to talk her into it for a couple of years and I don't think I'd have succeeded now if I hadn't threatened to join the Foreign Legion.'

'Is that thing still going?' Andrew enquired, but Josie explained.

'Les has got a job in Auckland, and we're flying out the weekend after next.'

'Congratulations,' said Andrew, but I could hardly take it in.

'New Zealand! What a terribly long way to go!'

'It won't take them all that much longer than it'll take us to get to Scotland, assuming we stop overnight at Kendal again.'

My mind was still boggling at the thought as we drove back.

'Well I've come a good long way from Colorado Springs,' Andrew pointed out. 'Anyway I expect she'll keep in touch with you. Airmail letters only take a few days.' He paused reflectively. 'And think of those guys that are going to ride in this rocket we're building, to Jupiter and back. That's about five hundred million miles each way.'

*   *   *

A few weeks after we got back from London there was the Spring Ball. It sounds like some sort of gimmicky mechanical toy doesn't it, but it was the high spot in the Station's social calendar. Some people maintained that it was instituted by the Director so that he could have a good look at the wives and girl-friends of his staff, and real dyed-in-the-wool cynics suggested that he wanted to hear what the staff had to say about the Station when their tongues were loosened by all the social lubricant dispensed gratuitously in the Station bar that evening.

People said all sorts of unkind things about the Director, but I found him very charming when Andrew introduced us.

'Good evening Dr Sanders. May I introduce my wife, Helen?'

'Good evening Mrs Garth. It's very nice to see you here. Dr Garth is one of our most respected young scientists, you know. We were very lucky to be able to entice him away from all the other more lucrative jobs he was offered. Are you enjoying the dance?'

I assured the Director that I was having a nice time and, after insisting that my champagne glass be refilled, he passed on to continue the spreading of joy and goodwill to other parts of his empire. Do I sound cynical now? Well of course my views are coloured by all that happened later on, but at that time I thought he was very charming indeed.

There wasn't actually a great deal of dancing at the Spring Ball. In the nineteen seventies, you remember, dancing was going through a rather peculiar phase. The old minuet, gavotte, and polka, which we are so familiar

28

with today, hadn't yet come back, and usually all there was to do was a sort of aimlessly frenzied jerking and shaking. At the Space Station they also went in for quite a bit of traditional Scottish dancing – because it was in Scotland I suppose, although in fact there weren't that many Scots on the staff.

Andrew and I tried all the Scottish dances; he'd borrowed a book from the library and memorized all the footwork with astonishing success. The only one we didn't have together was The Dashing White Sergeant, and I danced that one with Dr and Mrs Sanders.

'I do hope your husband will forgive my stealing you for just one dance, but this one's in threes isn't it, and I couldn't help noticing how gracefully you and Dr Garth perform these delightful Scottish dances.'

The Dashing White Sergeant didn't leave all that much opportunity for conversation, which was just as well because although I found the Director charming it was a bit overwhelming in a concentrated form and at such close range. We did exchange a few words during the less energetic moments.

'I have been told that you and your husband met through a computer selection agency.'

'Yes,' I said coldly. How the hell did he know that? I hadn't told a soul at Bannockside, and I felt sure that Andrew wouldn't have.

'That is very interesting,' Dr Sanders continued. 'I am a firm believer in the principles embodied in the method, and I think it will come to be much more widely used in the future.'

'It worked extremely well for us,' I informed him.

'Tell me Mrs Garth, was the selection based on an actual genetic study or merely on a community of tastes and interests?'

'We just filled in a form.'

He'd got a nerve, and I don't think anybody without his confident charm would have dared, but we abandoned conversation to concentrate on a slightly more intricate phase of the dance. During the next lull in the choreography Dr Sanders was talking to his wife, and when he turned to me again I filled in with rapid chatter about the band, the weather, the latest financial crisis, and the reported activities of various television personalities. Finally it was time for the Director and his wife to escort me back to Andrew.

'Thank you very much Mrs Garth. That was most enjoyable. By the way, I understand that you had to give up your teaching post in London to come to Bannockside with your husband. If you should find that time hangs too heavily on your hands I am sure that Mr Baron could find you a suitable post at the Space Station. We do not, of course, require any infant teachers as such, but possibly a position such as receptionist or librarian might prove congenial.'

'Thank you very much Dr Sanders, but I should prefer to stay at home and look after my husband.' I was hoping for something else to occupy me, but everyone told me you mustn't be impatient about these things.

*   *   *

It was also about that time that I joined the Station dramatic society. For a group supposed to be lacking a liberal education the space scientists were surprisingly keen on acting. Their wives were encouraged to join as well but on the whole they weren't as enthusiastic as their husbands.

When I joined they had already begun rehearsals for 'Uncle Vanya' but I was enlisted as assistant property mistress. Andrew wasn't a member but he encouraged me to belong; he said it was useful to have me out of the way one evening a week so that he could get on with the more messy jobs about the house.

The play was performed once in the Station canteen and once at the Women's Institute at Aberlochie, the nearest town. All the proceeds were in aid of Organ Donor

Appeals. Does that surprise you? I must admit it seems a pretty gruesome idea nowadays and with simple mechanical replacements available for most of the important organs there's no need for it. But it was all the rage around 1980 and there's no doubt that a lot of lives were saved and a lot of very sick people were restored to health by the transplant operations. The difficulty was finding enough donors and that's what the money was needed for – publicity. People were asked to sign a contract to say that when they died any parts of their body could be used in medicine, but they usually needed a bit of pushing before they could be bothered. Andrew and I had both signed; after all it was rather nice to think you could still help someone else even when you were dead, and the only inconvenience was having to give a biopsy sample for tissue typing.

But you'll be wanting to hear about the dramatic society. 'Uncle Vanya' was a great success, and I was surprised that Chekov should go down so well both with the Station staff and with the local people. The credit was due to Mrs Baron, the Personnel Manager's wife though. She was one of those producers with a magic touch; everything she suggested was just right, and her enthusiasm inspired every member of the cast. The assistant property mistress didn't have much to do, and I was hoping I might be given a slightly more responsible job in the next production. That was to be 'As You Like It'.

'Why don't you try for a part?' suggested Laura Wainfield, whose husband was in the Fuel Chemistry Department.

'It seems a cheek when there are so many people who've been members a lot longer than I have.'

'It's up to the producer to choose whom she wants, but anyway "As You Like It" needs quite a big cast. There's all those courtiers for one thing. I'm putting my name down for Phebe, the shepherdess. Well you can only try can't you?'

I didn't put my name down as a courtier; I applied for the part of Rosalind, and a few days later I had a note from the producer asking me to call at her house for an audition.

'Good afternoon Mrs Baron,' I greeted her when she opened the front door. 'I'm Mrs Garth and it's about the audition.'

'Oh hello Helen. Come into the sitting-room, and it's not Mrs Baron. It's Margaret to you. Now would you like sherry or gin?'

'Just a small sherry please. I'm sorry if I'm too early. How many others are coming?'

'There aren't any others this afternoon. I like to do all my auditions separately. It's most important to make a complete study of an actor or actress's total personality and you can't do that with everybody sitting round and mixing in together. Now let's just hear you read one or two of Rosalind's lines. I'll fill up your glass again first though so finish off that bit you've got left.'

I'd hardly started the first glass but I didn't like to protest that I could read much better sober, and Mrs Baron dispensed me another large glass of her sherry.

'I'd like to start by hearing you read Rosalind's long speech from Act IV, Scene I. You've brought your copy, have you?'

I put down my glass and swallowed hard. 'No, faith, die by attorney. The poor world is almost six thousand years old, and in all this time ... ,' I began. Mrs Baron was leaning back in her armchair with eyes closed. Dazedly I stumbled on to conclude, 'men have died from time to time and worms have eaten them, but not for love.'

Slowly Mrs Baron opened her eyes. 'She's a cynical bitch isn't she?'

'No she's not,' I protested. 'I like her.'

'And is it the fashion to see the lady the epilogue?'

'It is no more unhandsome than to see the lord the prologue,' I quoted. Mrs Baron chuckled. 'Yes. Full marks. You have done your homework. Now tell me how long you have had this desire to be a man.'

'I don't know what you mean.'

'Rosalind. For most of the play she is masquerading as

a man, Ganymede. And that's another thing. Do you know what Ganymede is?'

'He was Jove's page,' I told her.

'Not who, what. I mean the astronomical Ganymede, and I can see from the look on your face you don't know what I'm talking about. Ganymede is one of Jupiter's moons – could be the one they land on for all I know.'

I don't know whether it was the two large sherries or Mrs Baron's magnetic personality but my mind was like a whirlpool with disconnected ideas flying round, colliding, and bouncing in all directions. We were supposed to be talking about 'As You Like It', a light-hearted comedy, so where was all this psychology and astronomy coming from?

'Now tell me a little bit about yourself, Helen,' Mrs Baron said soothingly. 'For example, would you describe yourself as an adventurous person?'

'No,' I told her emphatically.

'And yet you left your nice quiet safe job in London to come up into the wilds of Scotland with a man from a far country, whom you had only known for a few weeks.

'Andrew and I love one another,' I told her angrily. 'That was enough.'

'But supposing your husband had wanted to take a job even further away – say New Zealand, like your friend Josie's husband. Would you have been happy to go with him then?'

'Of course I should, but how do you know so much about me, about my friends and their doings?' I demanded.

'I forget who told me about Josie Bernstein. It just came up in conversation somewhere I suppose, but please don't be so agitated, Helen. Sit down and have another drink. Would you like gin this time?'

'I'm afraid I have to go now, Mrs Baron. I'm sorry if you haven't finished the audition, but I don't think I really want to be in the play.'

I don't know what she must have thought but I just grabbed my coat and rushed out of the front door with hardly another word. So I didn't get the part, and I couldn't have done it anyway; by the time the play went on I was in no state to act in anything.

*   *   *

I'd almost got back to 'Tidal Cottage' when I met old Mr Campbell, the headmaster of the Bannockside Primary School.

'Good afternoon Mrs Garth. I was just on my way to call on ye.' He peered into my face. 'Are ye all right Mrs Garth? Ye look rather flushed.'

'It's all right,' I panted. 'It's the weather – very hot for walking.' In fact I had run all the way from the Station.

'Ye mustn't overdo it ye know,' he said solicitously. 'I don't suppose ye'll be used to these hilly parts, so ye want to take things more steadily.'

'I must,' I agreed. 'But what was it you wanted me about?'

'Ah yes. Just a wee matter. If ye'll permit me to walk back to your cottage with ye I'll be telling ye.'

'Certainly.'

' 'Tis young Miss Jamieson that has had to be leaving the school at the end of this term, and we canna get anyone to take her place. She has been a very foolish lassie. It was young Alan Renfrew up at the bakery, and they are going to be wed on Saturday week, but it's no way for two young people to start their lives is it? She will be leaving the school to look after the bairn.'

'I had heard about Elsie,' I admitted. 'I think they'll be happy together. Alan seems a nice lad. But why did you come to tell me about it?'

'We canna find anyone to take her place,' Mr Campbell explained. 'No one has answered the advertisement and I thought mebbe being a school-teacher yourself ye might care to help us out.'

We had reached the front gate of the cottage and I paused with my hand on the catch. Another month had passed, but surely it couldn't be long now. Why did conception have to be so much easier for girls like Elsie Jamieson who didn't want it?

'I'm sorry Mr Campbell. I should like to take up teaching again one day but I don't think I could manage it just at the moment. Would you like to come in for a cup of tea now we're here?'

'It's very kind of you Mrs Garth but I think I had better be getting back. I thought perhaps ye must have decided ye'd rather stay home to look after your man, and I expect ye'll be starting a family of your own one of these days. But if ye do ever want a teaching job I know I could find a place for ye. I ken well enough the sort of lassie that makes a good teacher and I'm sure you would.'

'It's nice of you to say so. I like teaching and I really am sorry I can't take Elsie's place.'

Mr Campbell said goodbye and I ran into the house, threw myself on the bed, and buried my face on the pillow. I don't really know why. Anyway two days later I had something else to worry about.

*   *   *

That Friday it was Andrew's afternoon for the Space Medicine tests, and he came home looking really groggy. Not just very tired as he had been before, but completely knocked up.

'I don't feel like any dinner tonight, Helen. I think I'll go and lie on the bed.'

'What's the matter Andrew? Are you all right?'

'It's nothing. Just slightly exhausted I guess.'

'Would you like me to ring the doctor?'

'No. There's nothing the matter, Helen. I just need a short rest. I'll be all right darling, honestly.'

'I'll bring you a cup of coffee then.'

I helped him up the stairs and went straight down to put the percolator on. As soon as it was ready I took Andrew a cup with three spoonfuls of sugar in, but he was fast asleep.

It seemed to be just a normal sleep, but perhaps he was

35

in a coma. How could you tell when someone was in a coma? I wasn't exactly sure what a coma was. I ran back down to the telephone. Should I ring for Dr Lowrey in the village, or should I try and get the Station surgery? What should I say was the matter? If only Andrew had told me what had happened to him. I ran back up to look at him again, but he just seemed to be sleeping normally. He looked just the same as every night; Andrew always fell asleep before I did because I used to lie awake and worry about things. I put an extra blanket over him and lay beside him with my book. I didn't read any of it though because I kept looking at Andrew to see if he were all right. I decided just to let him have his sleep out, but if he showed any signs of something the matter I would telephone Dr Lowrey straight away. At half-past nine he woke up.

'Andrew. Are you all right?'

'Yes of course. What time is it? Good heavens, half-past nine. I was a bit tired.' He sat up grinning cheerfully.

'Andrew. What happened to you this afternoon?'

'Nothing special really. We were on the G-machine mostly.'

'What's that?'

'It's just a sort of turntable with a swinging seat on it. The centrifugal force produces the effect of increased gravity, so the faster it goes the heavier you feel. When you get up to about four or five G you can hardly lift your arms up because they're so heavy.'

'Andrew!'

'Around eight or ten G you would black out, of course, but we didn't go as high as that.'

'Andrew. You must make them stop.'

'It's nothing to worry about, honey, though I must admit it's a bit tiring. I don't reckon I envy those guys in the Jupiter capsule who're gonna have to drive it under those conditions.'

'Is it a very high G on Jupiter then?'

'About three on the surface I should guess but I doubt that anyone will be going down there. Conditions would

36

be too hostile. They'll have to take all their readings from an orbiting vehicle, unless they land on one of the moons. No, the high G comes from the acceleration.'

That reminded me of something. 'By the way,' I asked him, 'what is Ganymede?'

'That's one of the moons. Why? Have you been studying astronomy?'

'No. It's a name in "As You Like It", and Mrs Baron said about it being a moon.'

'Fancy that. She's a smart dame is Mrs Baron. Not exactly an oil painting though is she? How did you get on in the audition, by the way?'

'I've decided not to try for a part,' I told him. 'I can't stand Mrs Baron.'

'I can see what you mean,' he admitted. 'I don't think I could. I sometimes wonder how Mr Baron does. But never mind. Let's forget all about the Station and have an early night.'

'Are you sure you feel all right now Andrew?'

'Right as rain.' His strong hands grasped my shoulders and he looked intently into my face. 'Would you like for me to prove it?'

'I think you ought to take things steadily after all those Gs.'

'You be careful what you're saying, young woman. I'm easily insulted you know.'

'We haven't had our dinner yet,' I reminded him.

'That's true. We'll have a quick dinner and then come straight back for half an hour's marital bliss.'

'It's all marital bliss, isn't it?'

'You know what I mean.'

'Well come and try my cooking first.'

We both laughed and ran downstairs together.

Afterwards we talked for a while, but quite soon Andrew closed his eyes and fell asleep with a look of peaceful content. For me the warm happiness was disturbed by nagging fears. Perhaps we should never have any children. Perhaps one of us was infertile. It must be me surely. We'd been married nearly two years and I did want children while we were still young. Perhaps I should see Dr Lowrey, but I knew he'd laugh and say there was plenty of time.

I had other things to worry about too. Why did everybody at the Station keep asking us such strange questions, and how did they know so much about us? And then there were the tests at the Space Medicine Department. I was terrified that something would happen to Andrew if they went on. If only I could persuade him to say that he didn't want to go on with it, but I knew he would never back out now. I would go and see the Director and tell him he must stop it.

* * *

Before I had plucked up courage to go and see Dr Sanders I had a message to say that he wanted to see me. Andrew explained:

'It's just some crack-brained scheme they've got, correlating job performance and motivation with personal relationships. Every man earmarked for promotion has to ask his wife to go along for a personality assessment test.'

'Does that mean you might be promoted?'

'Not necessarily, but I suppose it's a good sign.'

'They've got a bloody nerve all the same.'

'That's the way things are nowadays. The trend is all to more and more prying into everybody's personal affairs.'

'I think it's a dead liberty.'

'We might as well humour them though, since we've nothing to hide.'

'But supposing they don't like my personality. Supposing I don't come out very well and they decide not to promote you.'

'That is something I just can't conceive. What's the matter, honey? Did something upset you?'

'No. It's nothing Andrew.' Why did he have to use that word? Why did my worries all seem so mixed up with one another?

38

'Don't worry my love. I'll tell the Director I don't want you to have the test. They can't insist you know.'

'It's all right. I'll go. I'm not bothered about it.' At least if I went to see Dr Sanders it would be an opportunity to ask him to stop the Space Medicine tests. I would appeal to his better nature. I would threaten to write to our M.P.

*   *   *

'I must apologize for troubling you so,' the Director said as he showed me to one of the luxurious armchairs in his office. 'It really is terribly impertinent of us, and we're most grateful to you for helping us in our studies like this. You don't smoke, do you Mrs Garth? Now would you like a glass of wine?'

'I'd rather not, if you don't mind Dr Sanders.'

'Very well. We'll make a start on the formalities. It's a lot of red tape really but there's this questionnaire which Dr Randle has drawn up. He would have done the interviews but I thought that since you ladies were being so helpful in this matter the least I could do was talk to you myself. Now are you comfortable in that chair? Is the light too bright? Let me turn it down a bit.'

I was very comfortable in that chair. It supported me in a position that was neither sitting nor lying, more akin to floating perhaps. My face was inclined towards the Director, who sat alertly at his desk, his sharp black-bearded head silhouetted against a large pink disc of gentle light which constituted the room's only illumination.

'Yes I'm quite comfortable thank you.'

'Good. Then I'd just like you to answer one or two very simple questions.'

I should like to be able to tell you all the questions Dr Sanders asked me but I'm afraid I can't remember most of them. It started with my date and place of birth, the age of all my grand-parents when they died, my favourite colour, my favourite food, and my favourite drink. He asked me which historical character I most admired and I can remember saying 'Captain Scott', which is rather strange because I don't recollect ever having thought about him much before. I said the character I most despised was Ethelred, which is even stranger because I didn't know anything about him at all, and after that I was just conscious that I was answering questions but I wasn't aware what I was saying, not until the very end.

'Now Mrs Garth,' the Director was murmuring, 'just supposing there were another world very much like our world, but so far away that the journey would take ten, twenty, or perhaps thirty years. Supposing it were possible to build a space-ship to visit that world. Would you like to go on that ship?'

'Oh yes please,' I heard my voice saying, 'of course I would.'

Chapter five

I WAS terribly worried about it all, but when I told Andrew he just laughed.

'It's nice to know we shall have company on the trip,' he said. 'Yes I'm glad we're both going because it must be pretty lonely all those years out in space on your own.'

'Andrew! We aren't going anywhere. Andrew! We aren't are we? Tell me. I didn't really volunteer to go on a rocket did I?'

I think Andrew was a bit shocked at my reaction. 'No Helen. Don't worry. It was just joking honey. I've explained it to you. Nobody's going on a trip to the stars. It's just a personality test they've dreamed up. They probably try it on everyone to test their sense of adventure or something.'

'Are you quite sure?'

'Absolutely positive. They certainly won't get me on their rocket whether it's going to a star, to Jupiter, or even to the end of Brighton pier. I like it too much here. Besides I've decided I don't like all this messing about with gravity – one moment you've got about six G on, and the next minute you're weightless. You don't know whether you're coming or going, up or down or sideways. I like it with both feet on the ground. Helen darling. What's the matter?'

'I forgot to ask him. I was there in his office and I forgot all about it. All that business of the planet put it right out of my head.'

'What out of your head sweetheart? What did you want to do?'

'I'd made up my mind I was going to tell Dr Sanders he must not let you go on the G-machine any more. I was going to tell him he must stop it before something terrible happens, and then I forgot all about it.'

41

'It's not really anything to do with Dr Sanders.'

'He's in charge of everything.'

'Yes, but it's Dr Randle's job to select the volunteers for his tests. The Director wouldn't interfere in that.'

'Then I'll ask Dr Randle. I'll go and see him now and tell him it must stop.'

'Why don't you ring him up?'

I burst into tears. I thought Andrew cared more for me than to be sarcastic when he could see how upset I was.

'Helen my love.' He took me in his arms. 'I mean it. I'll telephone him shall I?' And I realized he was serious.

Two minutes later he was on the telephone and within another three minutes he was back telling me about it.

'It's all right. He doesn't need me for any more of the gravity experiments and he says he thinks I've done more than my share of the space medicine anyway. He's going on the gravity-simulator himself tomorrow.'

'I should have thought he would have tried himself before he risked anyone else.'

'He wanted to, but it wasn't really practicable because he had to work the monitoring equipment. Now that it's all recorded automatically he can go on himself.'

'Oh Andrew I am glad. I was really terribly worried you know.'

'I shan't be sorry to finish because it was taking up time I could have spent on my own research. You needn't really have been anxious honey. It wasn't dangerous, but I know you were worried and I hate to see you upset. I'm going in tomorrow for a medical check-up and then I'm finished.'

I flung my arms round his neck and without saying a word he swept my feet off the floor and carried me upstairs.

*   *   *

I said goodbye to Andrew next morning with a light-heartedness I had not felt for months and went back to clean right through the cottage.

42

In the middle of the afternoon the Station Rolls stopped by the gate, and the Director and the Personnel Manager came up the path. I opened the front-door and stood dumbly.

'Good afternoon Mrs Garth. May we come in for a few minutes?'

'Oh yes of course. I'm sorry. Good afternoon Dr Sanders. Good afternoon Mr Baron. Come into the front room and sit down.'

The two men seated themselves gravely in the two armchairs and I stood, still wondering what it was all about.

'Come and sit down Mrs Garth,' the Director beckoned. 'We have something very serious to tell you.'

I sat nervously on the edge of the settee. 'What is it? Is something the matter?'

'I am very much afraid there was an accident in the Department of Space Medicine this afternoon.'

'It was Andrew,' I gasped. 'Is he all right? Is it serious?'

I looked at my two visitors and their faces told me what they were still groping for words to express.

'He's dead isn't he? Andrew was killed. Well you might as well tell me.'

Mr Baron spoke for the first time. 'I'm terribly sorry Mrs Garth.'

'But he wasn't going any more – well only for a check-up. How can you get killed having a medical check-up?'

'The gravity-simulator machine went out of control,' Dr Sanders explained.

I saw red. 'You bloody murderers,' I shouted. 'Andrew told me he wasn't going on the G-machine any more. Why did you make him go again? And where's Dr Randle? It was his fault. He murdered my husband.'

The Personnel Manager spoke quietly. 'I am afraid that Paul Randle was also killed in the accident.'

'Oh my God! What was it? A bloody massacre? How many others were there?'

'Only the two,' said Dr Sanders. 'There will, of course,

be the fullest possible enquiry into the causes of the accident, but Mr Baron and I have established what happened from the reports of two technicians who witnessed it.'

'But he wasn't supposed to be on the G-machine,' I wept. 'He promised me he wasn't going on any more.'

'I think you had better let us tell you exactly what happened, as far as we have been able to ascertain,' said Mr Baron gently. 'Your husband was not on the gravity-simulator, and he should not have been involved in the accident at all. Dr Randle was on the machine and Dr Garth was just waiting for his medical examination.'

'What happened?'

'It appears that a small bolt fastening the turntable chair fractured and Dr Randle was thrown out of his seat. Eb rushed to his aid but just as he reached him the other side of the chair broke loose and they were both flung on the back wall.'

'Wasn't there any chance?'

'They were both killed instantly I'm afraid.'

The Director spoke again. 'Mrs Garth. I don't know whether it helps at all but your husband behaved with very great gallantry. He knew the magnitude of the forces involved and he virtually sacrificed his life in an attempt to save his colleague.'

'Thank you.' It didn't really help but they were doing their best.

'Would you like us to go now and leave you alone?' asked Mr Baron kindly. 'Or shall we stay with you a little longer? Would you like us to send someone to come and stay with you tonight?'

'Yes you can go now, and I don't want anyone else to come. I can manage all right thank you.'

'Later on, when you feel ready to discuss the future, we'll have another talk,' said Dr Sanders, 'but there's no hurry for that. Don't worry about anything Mrs Garth. The Space Agency will look after you.'

'Thank you very much,' I said coldly. 'I shall be all right thank you.'

I held the sitting-room door open and reluctantly and hesitantly they went out through the hall.

'Goodbye Mrs Garth and please do telephone us if there's any way at all in which we can help,' said Mr Baron at the front door.

'Thank you. I will. Good afternoon Dr Sanders. Good afternoon Mr Baron.'

I walked back into the sitting-room and sat on the settee staring at the carpet. What happened now? Nothing. There was no point in anything. That was the end. It had been nice while it lasted but it was all finished now. I wasn't worried about what would happen to me because I was just going to die. I wasn't going to commit suicide; I was just going to die because I had no reason or wish to stay alive.

Suddenly I had another thought. Perhaps it was a mistake, a case of mistaken identity. Perhaps it was a ghastly joke or perhaps it was a new personality assessment programme they had devised to test how I reacted to bad news. But I knew it wasn't that. I remembered the look on Mr Baron's face when they came in, and I knew that it was all horribly true.

*   *   *

I don't know how long I'd been sitting there like that when I looked up and saw Mrs Baron standing in front of me.

'I hope you didn't mind my coming in but the front door was open and you didn't hear my knocking. George asked me to call and see how you were,' she explained.

I stood up and tried to speak, but my throat muscles were rigid and unresponsive.

'No sit down Helen. Have you had anything to eat or drink? You poor girl. I'll make you a cup of tea in a minute.' She sat beside me and squeezed my hand.

Again I tried to speak, but a frozen paralysis had seized my tongue.

'It's all right Helen. Don't try to talk. Just relax. You'll

45

be all right. Now sit still here while I put the kettle on.'

She went out and I subsided again into wakeful oblivion until she came back with the little tray.

'Here now. Drink this and I think you'll begin to feel better. Let me steady your hand.'

I was trembling all over. I couldn't have held a cup of tea if my life depended on it, and Mrs Baron fed me like a child. Gratefully I felt the warm sweet liquid restoring my strength.

'Thank you Mrs Baron,' I said, my voice at least partly returning.

'Now I think we'd better get you to bed. You've had a dreadful shock and I'm going to ring up Dr Lowrey to ask him to come and give you a sedative. May I use your telephone?'

'There's really no need,' I protested, but Mrs Baron was already dialling.

'He's coming in threequarters of an hour,' she told me, 'and while we're waiting I'll just cook you an omelet.'

If I had had to make a list of people I should like to have with me at a really bad time I'm afraid the Personnel Manager's wife would have been very near to the bottom, but I should have been doing her a grave injustice. I honestly don't think I should have survived that night if she hadn't stayed with me. She didn't make a fuss about anything, or talk too much, or bother me, but she was just there, doing what was required. Mrs Baron slept in the spare room and in the morning she cooked breakfast for me and then went off to her own home.

'I think you'll be all right now, Helen. I've got to go and see how George and the children are. I've telephoned your friend Laura, and she's going to look in during the morning to see if there's anything you want.'

Paul Randle was cremated the following Wednesday, and Andrew was buried in the local churchyard; everybody said I should have had Andrew cremated, but I wouldn't. His brother Jeff flew over from Chicago to come to the service, and I had a very nice letter from his father. He was a widower who had married again and

46

lived in Denver now. A notice in the Aberlochie weekly paper said Andrew and Paul had died as a result of an accident, and the way it was worded most people would probably think it was a motor accident.

I went to stay with Tom and Laura Wainfield, and Dr Lowrey gave me some antidepressant tablets. They were pretty mild compared with today's happiness pills but I took one and all my troubles evaporated, so I threw the rest away. It didn't seem right not to mind, and I managed without them. After two weeks with Tom and Laura I felt well enough to go home and cope with life again.

*   *   *

I had a note asking me to go and see the Personnel Manager that Friday and he was as kind as his wife had been.

'Good afternoon Mrs Garth. How are you now? You're looking a lot better.'

'I feel better now,' I assured him.

'We've got everything arranged,' he informed me when I was comfortably seated in his office, 'and the Space Agency solicitors are going to handle all your legal problems. The Agency accepts full responsibility for your husband's death and they are suggesting a figure of a hundred thousand for compensation.'

'A hundred thousand pounds,' I repeated stupidly. I was astonished at the sum they offered, but completely indifferent to how much I received. What did it matter? What did anything matter?

'I realize that no amount can compensate for losing Eb,' said Mr Baron. 'He was a fine man and we shall miss him badly at the Station. Anyway we can see that you do not suffer financial hardship. By the way if you wish to arrange for your own solicitors to contest the offer the Agency would be prepared to get in touch with them, but quite frankly I don't think the courts would award any more than that.'

'No it's all right,' I said absently. 'I'm quite willing to

47

accept what you offer, and I don't want to have my own solicitor.'

Mr Baron looked relieved. He opened a drawer in his desk and took out a large and very official-looking document.

'If you would just sign this then, that's about all the formalities we need bother with.'

He indicated the place for me to sign at the bottom of the page and seemed surprised when I picked up the agreement and settled down for a nice long read.

'There's nothing you need bother about,' he assured me. 'It's just the usual legal red-tape you see.'

'I have to undertake that I will not under any circumstances reveal anything I know of events at the Bannockside Space Station.'

'That's reasonable, isn't it?'

'Yes I suppose so. And I undertake that after leaving Bannockside I will not return to this district for any purpose whatever.'

'Yes,' said the Personnel Manager, a little more doubtfully.

'But Mr Baron, I'm not leaving Bannockside. I live here and I like it here.'

He looked as if fate had dealt him a cruel and unexpected blow. Clearly he had not entertained the possibility that I might want to stay in Scotland.

'I'm afraid we had been assuming that you would go back to London. The Agency will pay all your removal expenses of course and we would do what we can to help you find accommodation.'

'I have no ties in London,' I told him. 'Although I have only lived in Bannockside for two years I like it infinitely better than a large city, and I intend to remain here for the rest of my life.'

It's strange that I was so emphatic. Perhaps it was just that I didn't like being pushed around, or could it be that somehow I sensed that my ties with Bannockside were a great deal stronger than they appeared to be? Do you believe in feminine intuition?

'Then I take it you are not prepared to sign this agreement.'

'I'm afraid not.'

'Oh dear.' Mr Baron was at a loss. 'I'm afraid we hadn't anticipated that complication. I think I'd better have a word with the Director. Would you mind waiting here while I go and see him? There are some magazines on the window sill.'

He was back before I had finished the first 'Punch', and was ushering me into the Director's office.

'Come in Mrs Garth. Sit down there. I'm sorry about all this mix-up. We should have realized that with your husband buried in Bannockside churchyard you wouldn't want to leave the district for a little while at any rate. But I'll tell you what I suggest. We can have him moved to a cemetery in the London area and the Agency will arrange everything and pay all expenses. You can select a suitable memorial stone and we will have it put up in the churchyard of your choice. Now how does that suit you?'

I gaped at him in horrified incredulity, utterly incapable of finding words to express my revulsion.

'Of course,' he went on, 'I realize that there may be other factors to consider. You must have made many friends here and you probably think you would be lonely in London. But I have telephoned the headmaster of the Bridge Road Infants' School and he says that you seemed to be very happy there. Most of the staff you knew are still there and he is prepared to give you your old job back with two extra years' salary increments. The school secretary is ringing round to find you a flat to live in, so you see everything would be just as it was before you left to come to Scotland. Now what do you say to that?'

'I am going to stay at Bannockside.'

The Director's face took on a harder look. 'You do realize that unless you feel able to sign this agreement the compensation which the Agency has offered you might be held up almost indefinitely. If the case goes through the courts it could be years before it's all settled.'

'That doesn't bother me,' I told him.

'But you are going to need the money to live on. How else can you manage?'

'I can get a job can't I? You said yourself that Mr Baron would be able to find me something.'

'Yes I believe I did, but of course it would be out of the question now.'

'Why would it? What difference does it make? Why are you trying to get rid of me Dr Sanders?'

'Mrs Garth! Of course we are not trying to get rid of you. We just want to do what is best for you, but the situation is very much more complicated than you realize I'm afraid. It really would be best if you went back to London and settled down at the Bridge Road Infants' School. I'm sure you'd be happy there.'

Chapter six

I RESOLVED to see Mr Campbell about a job at the local school at the first opportunity, but it was half-past four by the time I left the Space Station and it didn't seem fair to bother the Head when he was at home, so I left it until Monday morning. I was there outside his study when he came back from morning assembly.

'Good morning Mrs Garth. This is a pleasant surprise. How are you keeping now? Come in and sit down.'

I sat on the ancient and rickety chair reserved for the Headmaster's visitors and began to tell him what I wanted.

'I've come to say I'd like to accept the job you offered me Mr Campbell. Now that I'm on my own I need a job and I'd love to work at your school if you'll have me.'

Mr Campbell was silent for a long time and when he spoke he seemed to be searching very carefully for the right words. 'Yes Mrs Garth I think ye'd be verra well advised to look for a job. It would take ye out of ye self and give ye an interest in life. I should like fine to have ye at the Bannockside Primary but I dinna think we could manage to get the necessary permission.'

'But Mr Campbell, you offered me the job, and you said that any time I decided I wanted to go back to teaching you'd be pleased to have me.'

'Yes lassie, mebbe I did, but I'm afraid I was speaking a wee bit out of turn, exceeding my authority ye ken.'

'What do you mean?'

'All appointments have to be made by the Education Committee. They're the ones that decide these matters.'

'Should I write to them then?'

'Ay. Ye could do that.' Again the Headmaster seemed to be choosing his words very carefully. 'Ye could write to the Education Committee but I'm afraid ye would be wasting your time. They will not appoint ye to a teaching post in this area.'

'But why? What's the matter with me? Just because I'm a widow it doesn't make me a social outcast does it?'

'No Mrs Garth, of course not. It is nothing to do with that, but there are a number of important considerations which have to be borne in mind.'

'Such as?' I·demanded. I'm afraid my patience was wearing very thin.

'Well for one thing the members of the Education Committee are verra keen on native Scots teachers, especially in these country districts. I doubt verra much that they would appoint a Londoner in Bannockside.'

'Nonsense. You're just trying to put me off.'

'Look Mrs Garth,' said Mr Campbell, 'I have told you that I would like fine to have ye at my school·but I am afraid it is not possible. Why don't ye go back to London? There is a verra great shortage of teachers there and I am sure ye would be much happier among your own people.'

*   *   *

Andrew's insurance policies were enough to pay off the mortgage on the cottage and leave about a thousand pounds for emergencies, but that wouldn't last long if I used it to live on. Tom and Laura advised me to keep it for legal expenses in case I had to sue the Space Station for compensation, but somehow I couldn't face the thought of that. Arguing about compensation was like trying to put a price on Andrew's life. I supposed they would pay me the compensation eventually but I shouldn't spend any of it. Buying myself anything with that money would mean that I was profiting by Andrew's death.

The day after my fruitless interview with Mr Campbell I went to Aberlochie in the car to call at the Vocations Register, although it wasn't called that in those days. I forget what its proper name was but everybody called it the Labour Exchange. I didn't know how long I should be able to keep the car on. That depended on what sort of job I got, if any.

'Good morning madam,' the clerk greeted me politely. 'Could I just have your particulars please.'

I gave him all my particulars and told him I was a school-teacher but wanted something else for a change. If the Education Committee refused to employ me I was going to have to do something else, wasn't I? He seemed to think it was a little strange, but was prepared to do what he could.

'You'd really do best to stay in the teaching profession,' he advised me, 'but I suppose if you've decided you can't stand kids we'll have to find you something else. That shouldn't be too difficult. Hold on while I go and see what we've got. There's a chair there if you want to sit down.'

He disappeared through a little door at the back of his office and I sat waiting patiently for about fifteen minutes. Then he came back looking, I thought, somewhat embarrassed.

'Sorry to be so long but I've been talking to the manager about you.'

'Did he suggest anything?'

'Afraid not. There's nothing on our books at the moment even remotely suitable.'

'I'm willing to try my hand at anything,' I told him, 'and I am quite prepared to consider anywhere within about thirty miles.'

'There's just nothing I'm afraid. It's a very bad area for unemployment you know. Now if you were looking for a job in London, or even Birmingham or Manchester say, it would be a different matter, but in this part of Scotland there's just nothing.'

'Never mind. I'll try again next week.'

'There might be something come in, but I wouldn't bank on it. It's a very slack time of the year.'

*   *   *

I called at the petrol station on the road into Ban-

53

nockside and I suppose I must have looked a bit depressed. The old man in charge looked at me sympathetically.

'Dinna fash yersen lassie. It canna be as bad as all that.'

'It can,' I told him.

'Has your boy stood you up?' he asked. 'Now if I was about forty years younger I'd take ye out meself.'

'I can't get a job,' I blurted out.

'Ah that's a verra sad thing,' he agreed. 'I was on the dole meself nigh on three years when we lived in Glasgow. But now a fine lassie like yeself should be all right. If ye were a laddie there'd likely be a job for ye here. I've been trying to find a lad for yon pumps ever sin young Jock Renfrew left me to join the army.'

'Would you let me do it?' I begged him.

'It wouldn't suit a high-class lassie like you,' he said. ''Tis a dirty job, and long hours, and 'tis only twenty pound a week.'

'Please let me try.'

Twenty pounds a week wouldn't go far, but if I gave up the car I should be able to manage, and as much as anything else it was a matter of pride to defeat the Director's attempts to drive me away. I couldn't understand why he was so determined to get rid of me, nor how his baleful influence extended to Mr Campbell, the Education Committee, and even the Aberlochie Labour Exchange. Fortunately old Mr Fraser at the petrol station didn't seem to be included, or so I thought. Anyway, I started the following Monday and found the work much more congenial than Mr Fraser had suggested it would be.

There were two petrol stations at Bannockside, and the other one was nearer to the Space Station so most of the staff patronized that one. They gave trading stamps, which old Mr Fraser stubbornly refused to do, selling his petrol at a penny a gallon cheaper instead. Nevertheless a few of Andrew's old colleagues did come in from time to time. One afternoon I recognized the charcoal-grey Rover which Dr Sanders used for those informal occasions when he apparently thought the Station Rolls would be too ostentatious.

54

'Good afternoon Mrs Garth. What a surprise to see you here. I had been wondering if you had succeeded in finding suitable employment and I'm so glad you did. I must consider changing my allegiance.'

'I'm sure you'll find our petrol is better,' I assured him, and he drove off with a warm and friendly smile.

What happened next I think I half expected. It was in my pay-packet that Friday – a polite note informing me that owing to staffing rearrangements I had become redundant. Like all my persecutors Mr Fraser was a mixture of sympathy and embarrassment.

'It's none of my doing love. It's them up at Head Office.' It was the first time I knew that Mr Fraser had a head office; I had thought he was a one-man business.

*   *   *

I was absolutely furious and I think if I'd met Dr Sanders that evening I should have pulled his hair out by the roots. Fortunately I met Tom and Laura and they suggested a different course of action.

'Look Helen. The advertisement for the teacher at the school is in the "Echo" again this week. Why don't you make an official application for the post and see what that does?'

'It's no good,' I told them despondently.

'At least it might force them to show their hand a bit more.'

Written application had to be made to the Headmaster – so much for Mr Campbell's protestations that it was nothing to do with him – so I wrote a suitable letter and took it to his house the next evening. If he objected to being bothered with school matters in his own time that was hard luck, but I didn't care.

'Good evening Mrs Garth. Come in. I don't think you've met Mrs Campbell have you? Alice dear, this is Mrs Garth from "Tidal Cottage".'

'We've met in the shops and around the village but never been formally introduced,' Mrs Campbell explained.

We shook hands and engaged in a short discussion of the weather, then Alice politely withdrew. 'I expect it's school matters ye've come about and I've got a few wee chores in the kitchen so if ye'll excuse me now I'll leave ye to your business.'

'It's only a letter of application,' I explained, but she had gone.

The Headmaster looked uncomfortable, but this time he was not getting off the hook so easily; I was determined to get what I wanted.

'This letter, addressed to you, is a formal application for the vacant post of assistant teacher at the Bannockside Primary School, which was advertised in the "Aberlochie Echo". I should be grateful if you would give it proper consideration, and before you throw it in the waste-paper basket I will tell you that I am sending a copy to the Education Committee, another one to the National Union of Teachers, of which I have recently renewed my membership, and another to my M.P. Sir James Willoughby.'

'I'm afraid you're wasting your time lassie. As I've told ye before I'd like fine to have ye teaching at my school but it canna be.'

'Why not? Who's told you not to employ me? Who was it?'

Mr Campbell was silent.

'You needn't be afraid to tell me,' I went on, 'because I know. It was Dr Sanders, the Director of the Space Station, or should I say the grouse-packing station. Mr Campbell I'm surprised that a man like you, respected for his integrity and high principles, should stoop to be the lackey of a man like that, and should persecute a helpless woman just on the grounds that she has lost her husband.'

I was laying it on a bit thick I must admit, but at least it stung the Headmaster into giving me an answer.

'Mrs Garth, I am no man's lackey.'

'But you do what Dr Sanders tells you. You're like a monkey on a stick.'

It still makes me shudder to think how rude I was to poor Mr Campbell, but he took it all like a lamb. An upright man with an uneasy conscience is a pitiful object, especially when he is trying to excuse himself.

'I have never allowed myself to be influenced in a decision by Dr Sanders, or anyone like him. When ye first said ye would like this post he had already been here to tell me that I must on no account employ ye and I had told him very bluntly to mind his own business. He was free to choose his staff and I would choose mine.'

'Why didn't you give me the job then?'

'Because on Monday morning I received a letter from the Director of Education saying that for reasons which could not be disclosed Mrs Helen Garth was not to be employed in any school in the county of Ross and Cromarty. I must obey the instructions of the Director of Education,' he said lamely. 'In any case if I'd taken ye on they wouldn't have paid ye would they?'

'But why? What have they got against me?'

'I honestly don't know, Mrs Garth.'

'It must be Dr Sanders at the back of it. I know it must be him.'

'Very probably I should say,' observed the Headmaster, 'but ye can't do anything about it.'

'Don't bet any money on that,' I warned him. 'It's a bit late tonight now, but first thing in the morning I shall call on Dr Sanders.'

*　　*　　*

I was terrified about going to see the Director, but anger overcame my fear, and when he invited me into his office I discovered a very curious thing.

'Good morning Mrs Garth. Come in and sit down. I know you don't smoke. You won't mind if I do though, will you?'

He took a cigarette from the elegant wooden box on his desk and attempted to light it with an expensive-looking gold-plated table-lighter, but he seemed unable to judge where to hold the flame. His hands trembled and, fumbling, he spoiled one cigarette before he succeeded in lighting another. He was a bag of nerves; he was frightened of something, and when he looked up again I saw in his eyes that he was frightened of me.

'It's nice to see you again Mrs Garth. How are you getting on? Do you find your work at the petrol station congenial?'

'I don't because I've had the sack, as you very well know.'

'How unfortunate. I had no idea.'

'Look Dr Sanders. We're going to waste a lot of time if you insist on treating me like a child. I know that you are trying to drive me away from Bannockside, although I can't imagine why, and I'm determined you're not going to succeed.'

'You are completely mistaken.'

'Anyway I'll come to the point. I have decided I am not going to put up with it any longer. I insist that you write to the Director of Education, or whoever it is you have been working on, and tell him that I am to be given fair consideration for the teaching post at Bannockside Primary.'

'I don't know what you are talking about,' he blustered.

'You will do this because otherwise I shall write a full account of what I know of events at the Space Station and offer it to whichever daily or weekly paper will have it.'

'They wouldn't touch it you know.'

'Maybe "The Times" wouldn't, but I can think of at least one that would.'

'You would be liable to prosecution under the Official Secrets Act,' he warned me.

I shrugged my shoulders.

'It doesn't worry me. In fact I think it would be rather interesting. Furthermore I intend to send the full facts to a Member of Parliament who I think may be prepared to raise the matter in the House of Commons.'

'I am quite sure that Sir James Willoughby would not be a party to anything so injurious to the national interest.'

'I didn't say our M.P., Dr Sanders. I said an M.P. The one I had in mind was Mr Nigel Wood.'

The Director's face had been pale at the beginning of the interview; it was now ashen. 'Nigel Wood is in the pay of Soviet Russia. He will stop at nothing to injure the interests of this country and it would be a disaster if details of what we are trying to do at the Station fell into his hands.'

I was beginning to be very puzzled. The Director's alarm seemed quite out of proportion to any threat that I could possibly pose to him. After all what did I know about the Station? Only that they were building a rocket to go to Jupiter, but that had been in all the papers. Two men had been killed on the gravity-simulator but, disastrous as it had been for Andrew, such accidents did happen. I continued to press my advantage.

'Nigel Wood is a respected member of parliament. His constituents elected him by a very large majority and if your remarks were published he could sue you for heavy damages.'

Dr Sanders began to take a different line. 'Look Mrs Garth. The work we are doing at the Station will ultimately be of inestimable value to mankind, but the general public is very conservative. In the present climate of opinion it might be considered improper. People take a long time to adjust their minds to fundamental advances of that nature, and I beg of you not to imperil our work by any rash and unconsidered action.'

I hadn't the faintest idea what he was talking about now, except that he seemed to think I knew something which, in fact, I didn't know. But I had a strong conviction that I had won.

'Dr Sanders, since you are going to have to trust me why not accept the fact and let me stay here? That way I can be on your side.'

Wearily he acquiesced. 'I suppose you're right.'

'Thank you,' I murmured with relief.

'The situation will be very delicate,' he warned me, 'and in a few years' time it will become much more so. It may be extremely painful for you personally, and you will require all your resources of courage and fortitude to bear it. Events have taken a most unfortunate turn which we could not have anticipated when the decision was made. Why don't you go back and settle in London, Mrs Garth?'

'I am going to stay at Bannockside,' I said firmly, 'and I should be grateful if you would now withdraw all impediments to my getting a job here.'

'I will write to the Education Committee today,' he promised, 'and I will arrange for the Legal Department to draft a revised agreement for you to sign.'

'You needn't bother about that because I'm not going to sign any of your agreements.'

'Oh dear. You are being difficult. It will be absolutely essential for us to have your pledge of complete secrecy for at least the next twenty-eight years.'

I remembered what Andrew had told me was the projected date for the Jupiter shot. 'I give you my word that I will not reveal what I know about the Bannockside Space Station to anyone until the year two thousand and five. Do you think you can take my word?'

'Yes Mrs Garth I do, but you must give the same undertaking about anything else you may see or hear during that time. Will you do that?'

'Yes I also promise to keep secret anything I may learn about the Space Station in the future.'

That was the end of the interview, and I didn't realize how much it had taken out of me until I got home and collapsed in a quivering heap.

Two days later I had a letter from the Director of Education offering me a job at the Bannockside Primary, and by the same post I had a cheque for one hundred thousand pounds from the International Space Agency. I asked the bank manager to invest that for me – I couldn't bear to spend a penny of it. Of course it would have been different if we had had children. Achingly I wished I could have had a son to remember Andrew by, but even the wish made me feel guilty. Wasn't it selfish to want a fatherless child just to cure my own loneliness?

Chapter seven

IT WAS a very contented routine at the Bannockside Primary, and in a way I think I was as settled as I remember being at any time. My life was empty compared with the two years with Andrew but at least I had given up worrying now. Having nothing to lose, no hostages with fortune, I no longer worried what blows fate might have in store for me; I was content to live from day to day, enjoying life as it came.

The classes at the school were not too large even though they each spanned an age-group of two years. Old Miss Travers took the infants, I had grades one and two, and Roger Limpet had the nine to elevens. Mr Campbell didn't have a regular class but he did a lot of teaching nevertheless, taking one grade at a time in rotation. I don't think the children were as bright as at Bridge Road but they were certainly better adjusted. Having a smaller number made it easier to get to know them and to get to know their parents, who would often bring them or fetch them, or just call in to see how they were getting on.

When I say I was settled that doesn't mean that I didn't miss Andrew; I missed him terribly and I knew I always should. I did sometimes wonder whether I should ever get married again and I knew I ought to if the opportunity arose but I just couldn't imagine it. It wasn't that no one was interested in me. Three or four of the local men asked me out at one time or another and a couple of times I accepted, but I'm afraid I was a great disappointment to them.

I met quite a lot of people at the weekly whist drive I went to with Miss Travers, but while I was making new friends in the village I had almost completely lost touch with the staff and families from the Space Station. Except for Tom and Laura that is.

On one occasion Laura invited me to go to the Staff Dance with her and Tom. This had now become a monthly event, and was almost all traditional Scottish dancing apparently.

'You won't want me tagging along with you,' I told her. 'Three's a crowd you know.'

'Please come Helen. There'll be a lot of people you can renew acquaintance with, and I'm sure you won't be short of partners. If you have a few dances with Tom it'll give me a chance to rest my feet. He's got far more energy than I have nowadays.'

I hadn't really got anything to wear but I bought some cheap material in Aberlochie and made it up to the easiest-looking pattern they had in the shop. The result was better than I expected. Tom and Laura admired it when I met them in the entrance hall as we had arranged.

'You look delicious in that outfit,' said Tom while we waited for his wife to finish powdering her nose. 'If I weren't spoken for you'd arouse my animal passions in that.'

'It's very kind of you to say so,' I told him, embarrassed by the extravagance of his compliments.

'That's a super dress,' Laura commented when she joined us a few minutes later. 'You didn't buy that in one of our local boutiques.'

'I made it myself.'

Laura threw up her hands in mock despair. 'Did you? Well I can't compete with that. You've missed your vocation, haven't you?'

As we talked we were joined by a bald but athletic-looking man in a Lovat tweed and a tall black-haired woman in a white trouser suit.

'Do you know Alec and Shirley Teale, Helen? No I'm sure you don't. Helen this is Shirley and this is Alec. Shirley and Alec this is Helen.'

We continued to chat about nothing in particular as we drifted towards the staff canteen, where the dance was being held, and then the Teales moved off to greet some other friends.

'Where does Alec Teale work?' I asked Laura.

She hesitated a moment before answering, 'He's the new head of Space Medicine.'

'Taking Paul Randle's place,' I added.

'I'm sorry Helen. I didn't want to remind you but you asked about him.'

'It's all right. I don't have to be reminded; it's always there. I presume somebody has taken Andrew's place in Metallurgy, but the thought doesn't upset me. Anyway they're just starting another dance. You two give us all a demonstration. What did he say it was? The Rakish Highlandman?'

As soon as they'd gone somebody came and led me off into the galloping melee. I didn't know many of the Scottish dances but I had a go at several of them with a number of Andrew's old colleagues, and we seemed to get on all right. They were all very nice to me but I fancied their wives were just a little bit cool, although I don't mean impolite in any way. When I mentioned it to Laura she laughed.

'Yes you could be right. Considering how most of them treat their husbands it's not surprising that they consider an elegant and unattached female as a potential threat.'

'Laura! How could you say a thing like that?'

*   *   *

The next Friday we had a staff meeting at school. It was on 'Plans for the Future' but nobody seemed to know exactly what that meant. Anyway as soon as the children had all left we went along to the Head's study to be enlightened.

'Ladies and gentleman,' Mr Campbell addressed us, 'I don't want to keep you too long but I thought you would all be interested to hear about the Education Committee's plans for the future, and I would like to hear what ideas you have about our new school.'

We were slightly dumbfounded at that, although in the case of Miss Travers the affliction only lasted about five seconds. 'What new school?' she demanded. 'Nobody told me we were having a new school.'

'Nor should they,' said the Head, 'because the decision has not yet been made public, but I am informing ye officially at this verra moment.'

'It's not before time,' commented Roger. 'The ceiling's falling down in my class-room, but what's made that load of professional skin-flints decide to cough up now?'

'The members of the Education Committee have been concerned for some time about the dilapidated condition of the school buildings, but unfortunately the necessary funds have not been available.'

'And now they've come up on the Treble Chance,' suggested Roger. How he managed to get away with such a cheeky attitude I don't know, unless it was because he was a very good teacher.

'The Ministry have decided to make a special grant for new buildings so that we may be adequately equipped to deal with the sudden increase in our numbers in a few years time.'

I think we all looked blank at that. 'Why are we expecting a sudden increase, Mr Campbell?' I asked him. 'I thought the bulge in primary school places occurred some years ago.'

'This is a special little local bulge,' he explained, 'caused by the children from the Space Station.'

'The children of the Space Agency staff are here already,' said Miss Travers, 'but there are only six of them.'

'Exactly. And they fitted into our existing form structure without any difficulty. But you must realize that the staff at the Space Station have a very uneven age-distribution. It's a new organization and most of the staff joined it round about the same time and at the age of about twenty-five. So they'd either just been married a few years or were about the age when they might be thinking of getting married. Their first children will soon be old enough to start school.'

'I see,' said Miss Travers. 'And the children we have

already are from the few older members of the staff who had families when they came.'

'The new school is going to be on the Mallorchy Road about a mile from the end of the loch, where the Committee have an option on the land. It will be designed to accommodate a hundred and eighty children, more than twice the present number, with a staff of seven including the headmaster.'

'When will it be?' I asked.

'It is intended that we should be able to move in September of next year, but the plans have not yet been completed and I have been asked to send any suggestions for special facilities we would like.'

'We could do with a decent gym,' Roger suggested.

'And a proper library,' added Miss Travers.

'What about you, Mrs Garth? What would you specially like us to have?' Mr Campbell asked.

'Visual and aural aids I should say. We ought to have a film-projector with sound, and we could do with a cassette-television so that we could use the programmes when we liked instead of having to make our time-table fit in with the educational telecasts.'

'I am sure we shall have all those things,' the Head assured us, 'but I was really thinking of more revolutionary concepts.'

'A nuclear physics laboratory,' suggested Roger.

'Yes that's the sort of thing,' the Head agreed, apparently not noticing Roger's irony. 'Nuclear physics, biochemistry, organic synthesis, metallurgy, microbiology, all that sort of thing, with a special lab. for each subject of course.'

'Shall we be taking them up to eighteen now, then?' Miss Travers enquired.

'Oh no. Just five to eleven and then they go on to the new comprehensive at Dunburn.'

Miss Travers, Roger, and I could make no further contributions at that point and the Head went on.

'We shall only be doing the subjects at a very elementary level,' he explained, 'but you've got to realize that

65

these children can be expected to have a very high I.Q. and of course their parents will all be very keen for them to do well at school.'

I'm afraid none of us was able to suggest anything else, but Mr Campbell wasn't put out. 'Well now I expect ye'll be needing a day or two to let the ideas sink in, and I'd be grateful if ye'd let me know of anything else that occurs to ye. I myself have been wondering about a language laboratory but Dr Sanders says he thinks the Agency children will be more interested in science than languages.'

* * *

On Saturdays and Sundays I used to do a lot of walking in the hills and one morning, on the other side of the loch, I met Shirley Teale. She was the one I was introduced to at the Station dance, you remember, and her husband was the new Head of Space Medicine. She was being dragged along by twelve boisterous puppies, each on a separate lead.

'Are you going hunting?' I enquired.

'It looks like it, doesn't it?' she agreed. 'I'm just exercising some of Alec's dogs for him while Doris is on holiday. Doris is the girl in the Dog Unit, you know.'

'They're beagles aren't they? I think they're lovely.' I admired the puppies as far as possible without getting trampled to death, while they jumped up and showed their delight at finding a new chum by licking me all over.

'Did you say some of Alec's dogs?' I asked.

'Yes I've promised to take the other twelve out this afternoon. This is all I can manage in one go,' she added, a statement whose truth I could hardly have disputed.

'Forgive my asking but why does your husband want so many dogs?'

'I don't exactly know. They aren't his personally of course; they belong to the Space Station. I suppose they need a large number so that the experiment will be statistically significant.'

'Experiment?' I was horrified at the picture of those charming puppies being tortured in the lab.

Mrs Teale laughed. 'Don't look like that. They don't cut them up or do anything to hurt them. You can see how happy they are, and they all adore Alec.'

'What do they do then?' I insisted. 'Do they put them on the G-machine, or are they going to send them up in a rocket?'

'I'm sure they don't do anything like that. As far as I know they just observe them. They were all bred at the Station so I suppose it's really what you would call a genetic experiment.'

I stroked two eager warm heads. 'What are they called? Have they all got names Mrs Teale?'

'They've all got names, and Doris can tell them apart, but I can't. They're all bitches by the way. That's a funny thing isn't it. Alec says females are easier to handle and more amenable to discipline. I wonder what the Women's Lib. Movement would think about that.'

'They must be all the same litter,' I said, 'but twenty-four, how can they be? And all the same sex. It certainly ought to go in the Guinness Book of Records.'

'I don't think it would qualify for that.' She smiled enigmatically. 'But I shall really have to get on with their walk before they pull my arms out of their sockets.'

I watched them drag her off along the shore of the loch. I hadn't thought that even puppies from the same litter would be as much alike as that. Perhaps it was a very pure breed.

*   *   *

I still had the Mini and it wasn't showing any particular signs of age, but there were bound to be little things go wrong from time to time and I could never tell how serious it was. I used to take it for a regular service at Black's garage at Aberlochie and I fitted that in during the school holidays but when anything else went wrong I had to take it over one evening, come back on the bus, and fetch it the next day. One time, for example, it started making a noise like a jet aircraft; Roger Limpet said he thought it had a hole in the silencer.

I had left the car at Black's and was waiting at the bus-stop, trying to shelter from the driving rain behind my fashionable tiny umbrella, when I recognized Tom Wainfield in his new Italian car. He stopped by the kerb and I hopped in gratefully.

'I've just taken the car to Black's,' I explained, 'but I didn't pick a very good day for it.'

'It's an ill wind,' he replied. 'Now I've got company on the way home.'

I didn't actually like the way Tom drove; I suppose he was safe enough but he certainly went round bends a lot faster than I did. The road was awash with water at first but about five miles out of Aberlochie the rain suddenly eased and within a few minutes the sun had come out. It was just where the road crossed the river and as we drove up and over the bridge there facing us was the most magnificent double rainbow you could imagine. Tom turned the car off the road by the clump of trees on the left, hidden from the Aberlochie side but with a view along the valley to Bannock Loch. The two arcs of colour, one brilliant and one fainter, framed the picture of the river.

'I've never seen a rainbow like that,' I said.

'Worth stopping to admire.'

As we watched the colours even deepened in intensity but then, almost imperceptibly at first, began to fade.

'Why don't you take your coat off? It's wet through and the heater's warmed the car up now. I put it on full when you got in.'

Tom helped me off with my coat, a slightly awkward operation in the front seat of a car, then reached to feel the collar of my blouse.

'Is this wet as well?'

'I'm afraid so, but I'd better keep that on hadn't I?'

His hand rested casually at my throat and suddenly his fingers became charged with electricity. Sensing my response he allowed his hand to slide slowly downwards and moved his face towards mine.

'You know you're very beautiful, Helen.'

With a reluctance which shocked me I lifted his hand and pushed it away. Casually it fell on my thigh, its electric charge no less devastating. Terrified, of myself more than of Tom, I grabbed his hand and placed it on the steering wheel.

'The rainbow's gone now Mr Wainfield, and I think we should go.'

'Don't be like that Helen darling. I didn't think you were that sort of a prude.'

'I don't know what you thought, but whatever it was you were dead wrong. I certainly don't make a habit of having it off with my friends' husbands in the back seat of their cars. Or the front seat,' I added for the sake of accuracy.

He still hadn't given up hope. He must have been pretty stupid, or perhaps it was that having committed himself he thought he might as well keep trying. 'I'm sorry Helen. I should have known. But we could go away somewhere, just the two of us, one weekend. How would that be?'

'Look Mr Wainfield,' I told him. 'When these randy fits come over you why don't you ask your wife if she can help? Or else get a nice strong sedative from the doctor.'

That seemed to sober him up. 'Laura doesn't want to know,' he muttered, 'but it doesn't matter. I'll find someone else.'

Without another word he started the car and drove at an even faster speed than before to the door of my cottage.

'Thanks for the lift, Tom,' I said as I got out. 'I shan't tell Laura that we stopped to look at a rainbow.'

*   *   *

I didn't mention it to Laura but it was soon obvious that Tom was very far from the devoted husband I had at one time imagined him to be. I used to call and see Laura about one evening a week, or sometimes she would visit me. She had recently become interested in dressmaking and I used to help her. It was clear that she didn't see much of Tom in the evenings, and we hardly spoke of him. She seemed to be looking around for other interests.

'Can you play bridge?' Laura asked me one day.

'I never have done, although I vaguely know the rules,' I admitted. 'I play in the village whist-drive every week with Miss Travers. Why?'

'I was just thinking that if you learnt we could have a game at Jack and Angela Noble's sometimes. Tom and I used to play with them but he's always too busy nowadays.'

'I'm willing to have a try if you'll teach me.'

So it was agreed, and after a couple of two-handed practice sessions and a lot of discussion about the bidding we ventured out to do battle with Jack and Angela. The Nobles lived quite near to Tom and Laura in a Space Agency house similar to theirs but slightly larger. Jack was in the Electronics Department.

Jack and Angela were not as good as Laura but better than I was so the games were reasonably even. They were constantly interrupted by Angela going to see why the babies were crying. If they were quiet for too long she would go to see why they weren't crying.

'Can I come and have a look at them?' I asked her.

'Of course. Be careful how you open the door,' she whispered. It was one of the occasions when they weren't crying.

Cautiously we tiptoed into the bedroom and I looked at the two cots, one adorned with blue ribbon containing a beautiful golden-haired child of about eighteen months, the other decorated in pink and carrying a less attractive red-faced baby with meagre brown hair. Inexperienced as I was in such matters I judged the girl to be about a year old, and I found the fact slightly baffling.

'They're lovely,' I whispered. 'Are they twins?'

'They don't look it, do they?'

'They don't even look like brother and sister,' I admitted.

'I'll tell you about it downstairs,' Angela whispered, and we tiptoed back to the sitting-room.

70

'John is our own you see,' said Jack, as if that explained everything.

'What about the other one?' I asked diffidently.

'Oh Anne is from the Evercare,' Angela explained.

'The Evercare?'

'The Evercare Home. It's an orphanage, that place on the Inverness Road, about seven miles from Bannockside. We'd just had John when we had the letter from Matron asking if we would take Anne.'

'Why did she ask you in particular?'

'I think they wrote to everybody at the Station. It was a bit inconvenient, coming so soon after John but since there were so many children to be fostered out we didn't like to refuse. Dr Sanders said that everyone who could ought to make an effort to help. Anyway she'll be a playmate for John.'

Afterwards I asked Laura if she and Tom had been asked to take a child from the orphanage.

'We did get a letter,' she said sadly, 'but Tom wouldn't entertain the idea.'

Chapter eight

I HADN'T touched a penny of the compensation and I hadn't even bothered about how it was invested. Mr Ogilvy, at the bank, had seen to it and I had told him I wanted all the interest and dividends to be reinvested. The day after the visit to the Nobles I had my six-monthly statement, and for the first time I took the trouble to have a proper look at it. The original one hundred thousand had grown to almost a hundred and fifty thousand. I still didn't want to spend any on myself but I suddenly wondered whether I ought to give some away. To whom? What about the orphanage Angela Noble had mentioned? I resolved to visit the Evercare Home that weekend; I wasn't going to give them any of Andrew's money unless it seemed to be a reasonably well-run place.

*   *   *

'We don't get many visitors,' the Matron told me, 'so the poor wee bairns will be pleased to see a fresh face.'

Miss Anderson was a large red-faced grey-haired woman dressed in a spotless maroon and white uniform of exceptionally stylish cut. The small blonde nurse to whom she introduced me was also immaculately attired, but in navy-blue and white.

'This is Sister Baird, my right-hand woman. Sister, this is Mrs Garth, who has come to see whether there is any way she can help our bairns.'

'We always welcome anyone who takes an interest in them.' Sister Baird was staring at me. 'But haven't we met somewhere Mrs Garth? I feel sure your face is familiar.'

I searched my memory. 'I'm sorry but I don't think I

remember you. Maybe it was someone like me. People say I'm a very common type.'

I'd never been round an orphanage before so I hadn't got any standard for comparison, but the Evercare Home certainly surprised me. There were about forty children, all very young, in delightful little cots, two to a room. The rooms were bright and warm, luxuriously equipped and exquisitely decorated, each in a different colour; each room had one cot trimmed with pink and one with blue.

'This is Stanley,' said the nurse. 'He's one of the oldest ones we have left, and this is his sweetheart, Edna. Say hello to the kind lady Stanley. She's come to see how you're getting on.'

Stanley responded with a smile which broke my heart. Why could Andrew and I not have had a child like that? Why had I had to lose Andrew? Why could we not have had one another just a little longer? My troubles flooded back, the lemon-coloured walls began to rotate, and I realized that only Sister Baird's steadying hand was keeping me from falling.

'Would ye like to sit down Mrs Garth? Sit here and I'll fetch ye a nice cup of tea. I know it can be verra upsetting to think of the poor wee fatherless bairns. But they're verra happy while they're here. We look after them fine ye ken.'

I was too ashamed to admit that my distress was from pity for myself rather than for the children, and after a delicious cup of tea I was myself again.

'I am sorry to be such a nuisance, but I'll be all right now. May I say hello to the other boys and girls?'

Their ages ranged from about nine months to two years and they were as different as you could imagine. One little girl had bright red hair and green eyes, the next one golden hair and blue eyes, a third black hair, a fourth dark brown. I thought the girls were rather plain on the whole, but the boys were all very good-looking. Although they had every imaginable shade of hair and eye colours each one had the same captivating smile. Sister Baird said it was the wind but I didn't think it was.

73

Matron said goodbye to me in her office.

'Thank you for coming to see us Mrs Garth. It's always nice to know that our work is appreciated.'

'Thank you for having me,' I paused, hesitating with embarrassment. 'Matron . . .'

'Yes Mrs Garth?'

'There's something I wanted to ask you.' I hesitated again and then blurted out my request.

'Matron. Would you allow me to make a donation towards your expenses?'

'That is extremely kind of you and most generous. I'm afraid we can't accept your offer though because our constitution specifically forbids us to receive private donations.'

I was astonished. 'But all that wonderful equipment must have cost a fortune. And your running expenses must be enormous.'

'We do have a large budget,' she admitted, 'but all our basic requirements are covered by a grant from the Ministry, and the little luxuries come out of generous donations from local industry.'

There wasn't all that much industry round there but when I enquired which firms it was, Matron changed the subject.

'The Chairman feels that it would be unfair to accept contributions from private individuals because the Home will be closing at the end of next year.'

'Why is that? What will happen to the children?'

'They will all have been adopted by then. The Home was only intended to be open for a period of about three years, until the children were old enough to be cared for by adopted parents, and to allow us to find suitable homes for them all. We are verra verra careful in choosing families for adoption.'

It seemed a very funny business. I could appreciate that the children would be happier adopted, and part of an ordinary family, than in even such a beautiful institution as the Evercare Home. But how could they be sure there weren't going to be any more orphans coming along when

74

these had been settled? Matron admitted that she didn't know. Anyway I had something more important to ask about.

'Are you still trying to find homes for some of the babies?'

'Why yes now. I believe there are about a dozen still unaccounted for.'

'Matron. Do you think ... Would you possibly consider me do you think? Could I adopt one of these babies?'

'I dinna ken. It would have to go through the proper channels ye understand and ye must realize the Committee are verra verra careful.'

'How could I apply then?'

'Ye would have to obtain a proper application form by writing to the Chairman and then if ye filled it in and sent it back the Committee would consider your case. Write to the Chairman of the Management Committee, Evercare Home, Inverness Road.'

*   *   *

I sent the letter off that night, and while I was waiting for an answer I thought a lot about the babies. It had been an impulse asking to adopt one, but the more I thought about it the more important to me it became. Impatient for a reply to my letter, I met the postman at the gate every morning that week but always it was the same odd bill or circular he brought, until about ten days later he handed me an expensive parchment envelope with the word "Evercare" embossed in the corner. I could hardly wait to carry it back indoors before tearing it open and reading the single sheet of elegant headed notepaper.

'The Management Committee regrets that you are not eligible to be considered for adoption of a child from the Evercare Home.'

It was signed 'Gerald Lambert, Chairman'.

Dazed, I sat on the chair in the kitchen and let my shoulders flop on the table. I suppose I had known they might refuse, but I hadn't admitted it to myself.

Everybody in the papers, on the video, and on the radio talked of how it was perfectly possible for one parent to bring up a family, but when the chips were down they didn't really believe it did they?

But I wasn't going to give in without a fight, and I went straight from School that afternoon to call at the orphanage.

'Why hello Mrs Garth,' the Matron greeted me. 'It's nice to see you again. Have you come to watch the bairns have their tea?'

'I should like to see Mr Lambert,' I told her. 'Can you give me his address please?'

'The Chairman's office is here in the Home, but I don't think he's there at the moment.'

She led me across the thickly carpeted entrance hall to a heavy oak door with a small bronze antique knocker on it. Two taps on this produced no response so the Matron opened the door a few inches and peeped in. I got the impression she didn't want me to see in but I had a brief glimpse of opulent luxury before she closed the door.

'As I thought Mrs Garth, the Chairman is not here at the moment but I'm sure he would be delighted to see ye on some other occasion.'

'I'll make an appointment,' I suggested.

'No I'm afraid that's not possible. The Chairman's secretary keeps his appointments diary and she is not here just now either, but I will tell him ye called and I expect he will write and ask ye to call again some time when he's free.'

It wasn't very likely that I should be hearing from Mr Lambert, and as I set off for home in the car I tried to think what I could do next, but there didn't seem to be anything very promising.

About a mile down the road I passed Dr Sanders in his grey Rover heading towards Inverness and I suddenly had the ridiculous idea that he might be going to call at the orphanage. I turned at the next farm entrance to follow him and of course the Rover was out of sight, but I still half expected to see it parked on the broad semi-circle of gravel in front of the Home. That's exactly where it was.

I stopped the Mini half-way up the drive, my mind in a turmoil. What business did the Director of the Space Station have at the Evercare Home? Was his the local industry that contributed so generously to the Home's funds? And if so why? Even more preposterous ideas flashed through my mind. Were the babies from the Space Station? Were they children of members of the staff, orphaned in a ghastly accident inside that barbed-wire perimeter fence that had slaughtered their mothers and fathers in some dreadful technological holocaust? I knocked on the front door again, without any idea what I was going to say.

'I'm sorry to bother you again Matron but I saw Dr Sanders' car on the drive and I wondered whether that meant that Mr Lambert is here now.'

The Matron looked at me very hard. 'The Chairman is here now and Dr Sanders is in his office, but he will not be able to see ye.'

'I don't mind waiting until he's free,' I volunteered, not very hopefully.

'Dr Sanders will be there some time I'm afraid so it's really no good your waiting. You go home and I'll tell the Chairman ye called.'

In the gentlest and politest possible way she practically pushed me out of the front door.

*   *   *

The more I thought about it the more peculiar it seemed. For a start I was sure that Mr Lambert must have been there all the time when I first called. Then another idea occurred to me and I searched for the letter I'd had from Dr Sanders about the compensation. I'd still kept it, and I compared the signature with that of Mr Lambert's on his letter giving me the thumbs down over adoption. You didn't have to be a handwriting expert to see significant resemblances, and the implications of that staggered me. It was three days before I managed to work out that the next step was to telephone the Station.

'I'm terribly sorry Mrs Garth,' the secretary explained, 'but the Director doesn't have time for private interviews. If you have some personal difficulty on which you would like advice I could arrange for the Station Welfare Officer to call on you. Since you are the widow of an ex-member of the staff we would naturally like to help you in any way we can.'

'I wish to see Dr Sanders,' I insisted, 'but if I cannot make an appointment with him perhaps you would be good enough to arrange for me to see Mr Lambert.'

'I'm afraid I don't know what you are talking about.'

'You know very well what I'm talking about. I am referring to the fact that Dr Sanders and Mr Lambert are one and the same person.'

'Perhaps I had better see if the Director can speak to you on the telephone.'

'You do that,' I told her, and she did.

Dr Sanders came on the phone at once. 'Hello Mrs Garth. It's nice to hear from you. How are you getting on at school? Now when would you like to come and see me? Would half past four this afternoon be convenient?'

*   *   *

I went straight from school, the guards waved me through the main gate, and the commissionaire took me to Dr Sanders' office.

'Well now Mrs Garth. I have an idea that you have come to see me about something which is rather important to you.'

'I want to adopt a child.'

He looked at me and I felt he was wondering what line to take. 'You would like to adopt a child? Yes I can understand that, and I am sure you would make an admirable parent. But how should I be able to help? Do you wish me to give you a testimonial? I understand there is a great shortage of children for adoption.'

'I want a baby from the Evercare Home.'

78

'Evercare? Yes that is the name of the children's home on the road to Inverness, isn't it? Are they looking for homes for some of their children? Well you fix it all up with them and tell them to write to me for a testimonial.'

'I want you to fix it all up, Mr Lambert.'

He laughed good-humouredly. 'Perhaps we had better put our cards on the table. I accept that you know a great deal more than is good for you, but surely you must realize that it would be quite out of the question for you to adopt one of those children.'

'I know one-parent families are at a disadvantage,' I admitted, 'but plenty of widowed mothers bring up their children perfectly satisfactorily, to say nothing of abandoned wives and unmarried mothers. And I am financially independent. I haven't spent a penny of Andrew's compensation but I would gladly use it to live on if I gave up my job to look after a child.'

'Look Mrs Garth. I agree that you are quite capable of bringing up a child, but not one of these children. Surely you, of all people, must realize that.'

I was just about to ask him what was so special about these children when I suddenly realized that he thought I knew. Whatever it was, he thought I knew all about it and it was going to pay me to let him keep thinking just that.

'I have thought about it carefully Dr Sanders, or is it Mr Lambert, and I would like to adopt one of the babies. You might as well agree to it now because I shall give you no peace until you do.'

'I am quite prepared to believe that,' he said. 'I am well aware of your strength of character. Well I can't say I think it's wise, but we at the Station are deeply conscious of the debt we owe you and your late husband, so I am prepared to make arrangements for you to adopt one of the little girls.'

'It was a boy that I wanted,' I told him.

'But that would lead to even greater difficulties, wouldn't it? Just think of the problems that would arise with one of the boys. And the girls are such sweet little things.'

'Please let me adopt one of the boys. I promise to bring him up exactly as if he were my own son.'

The Director pondered. 'Yes. If you promise that, and if you swear to remember that at all times – exactly as your own son – I think I can agree.'

'Oh thank you thank you thank you Dr Sanders. I do promise. I do I do.'

It was all I could do to keep myself from throwing my arms round his neck and kissing him.

'Right then. If you will excuse me I'll fetch the necessary forms and we'll get everything signed up.'

He was only out for a few minutes but it was long enough for me to give way to my curiosity about something I had noticed when I first came into the room. It was a large oak-framed photograph lying face down on the desk and the moment the Director had closed the door behind him I picked it up and looked at the front. For what seemed an eternity I stared at the familiar face, then imagining I heard a footfall I hurriedly replaced the picture and rushed back to my chair. I was still trembling when Dr Sanders came back with the forms.

'Yes I think we've got everything here Mrs Garth. It's not quite the usual adoption arrangements, by the way, because I am remaining the legal guardian of all the children, and naturally they must be brought up in this district.'

'The last agreement you wanted me to sign was to say I'd leave and not come back,' I reminded him.

Again the Director laughed. 'That's quite true, but the circumstances are slightly different now, aren't they? You know you're a very clever woman Mrs Garth.'

All the way home I thought of the darling son I was going to have and the tears of joy made it difficult to see to drive. There were a lot of things I didn't understand though. One was why Dr Sanders should be so interested in me. I was sure he wasn't a secret admirer of mine so why should he keep my photograph in a place of honour on his desk?

Chapter nine

RICHARD WAS exactly like the son I would have wished for Andrew and myself. We could never have had a child exactly like him because he had fair hair and blue eyes and Andrew and I both had brown hair, but I was sure he had Andrew's smile. I don't know what his surname was originally but it was arranged that from then on he should legally be known as Richard Garth. He was eighteen months old when I had him and I left school at once to look after him. I didn't mind using Andrew's money to bring up Richard because I was sure he would have wished it. Mr Campbell was very good about my leaving.

'Of course it's all right, lassie. We'll manage, and when ye come back to teaching in a year or two we shall mebbe have our fine new building.'

'I don't think it'll be as soon as a year or two, Mr Campbell.'

'I wouldna be too sure about that now. A lassie that's a born teacher like yourself wouldna want to be out of the profession any longer than she needed.'

'I shall be busy looking after Richard,' I told him.

'Only until he's three.'

'What do you mean, Mr Campbell?' I said, suddenly alarmed.

'I just mean that our new school is having a fine nursery department and I have been told the authorities anticipate that by the end of the year every bairn in this district will be starting school at the age of three.'

'Well we'll see about that when the time comes.'

*   *   *

The time came incredibly quickly and a year and a half had flashed by almost without my noticing it. Perhaps under different circumstances I shouldn't have made such a full-time job of looking after one small child, but Richard had become my whole life; it seemed that every waking moment was devoted to him. It wasn't that he was specially demanding, and I hope I didn't spoil him, it was just that I needed someone to lavish my affection on. I was deliriously happy but I think I had lost my carefree composure of the last few years. Now I had something to worry about; I had gained a happiness which I knew I might lose in some way; I had given another hostage to fortune.

When Richard started at the nursery school I didn't know whether to go back to teaching myself or not. Mr Campbell had offered me a job but of course I was financially independent; I didn't need to work. The first few days at home watching the clock until I could go and meet Richard from school made my mind up. I should have to get a job to occupy myself all day.

All the children from the Evercare Home had been adopted by people living at Bannockside, most of them from the Space Station. Richard was the youngest, so by the time I went back to the Bannockside Primary they had all started in the nursery department. In the three forms which contained them they must have constituted about half the intake, but you couldn't tell which they were, not at that stage anyway.

For his third birthday I bought Richard a dog. You might not think a three-year-old would know what he wanted for his birthday but this one did, and he even knew which breed, although he didn't know the name.

'I want a doggie, Helen. I want a gold doggie with floppy ears like Mr Mac'tosh's.'

Mr MacIntosh lived at the other end of our row of cottages and his ears were quite normal but he did have a golden Cocker Spaniel bitch and he promised us we could have a puppy from the next litter. Richard had to wait a little while for his present but he didn't mind and he took a great interest in the expectant mother as the puppies' E.T.A. drew near. When at last the happy day came and the puppies were old enough to be inspected Mr MacIntosh said we could have first choice of the five little cuddly balls of bright-eyed life.

'I have this one, Helen,' Richard informed me. 'He called Butch.'

He had got the name from a video-tape cartoon but Mr MacIntosh apparently didn't think much of it.

'That wouldna do for a female now, but mebbe your mither'd like better for ye to have a dog-puppy.'

I wasn't bothered, so we had the little bitch and Richard agreed to call her Goldie. I fully expected that after a few weeks his interest would peter out and I should be left to look after her, but I was wrong; he immediately become devoted to Goldie and remained so all the time we had her.

* * *

Life at the new school was very different from what it had been at the old one. No expense was spared for equipment, the staff common-room was four times the size of the old one, and Mr Campbell's office was absolutely vast. His wall-to-wall carpet alone must have cost a fortune. There were seven teachers now and about two hundred children, but there was still the same friendly atmosphere.

We had to leave Goldie at the cottage while Richard and I were at school but Mrs McGregor next door used to keep an eye on her for us. When we got home Goldie would come bounding out to meet us and we would take her straight for a run by the loch. That was where she picked up the thorn. I noticed she was limping when we got back and found the thorn and pulled it out. Richard and I bathed her paw and I thought by the next day she'd be none the worse. She was still limping in the morning though and when we got back from school that day the paw had swollen to twice its size.

'We'll take her straight to see old Mr Pleasance,' I told Richard. 'He'll soon make it better.'

Mr Pleasance's surgery was about a mile down the road and we joined a short queue of people and animals in the dingy waiting-room.

'Tortoise,' exclaimed Richard, pointing admiringly at Sally Grantham's pet. 'Is tortoise poorly?' he enquired.

'I don't know what's the matter,' Sally's mother told us, 'but he seems to have no life in him at all.'

I thought it must be rather difficult to tell with a tortoise but I suppose its owner would know. Anyway Sally went in next, and a few minutes later it was our turn.

'Next patient please,' boomed a voice that I didn't recognize, and when we went in I saw that it wasn't Mr Pleasance at all. I must have looked a bit put out I suppose.

'Good evening. I'm George Bradwell and I've taken over the practice. Mr Pleasance retired at the end of last month and I've taken his place.' The speaker was a large cheerful outdoor-looking man of about thirty, with ginger hair and bushy eyebrows.

'It's Mrs Garth, and Richard, and Goldie,' I introduced us but Mr Bradwell was already examining the infected paw with an unexpected gentleness.

'That must be very painful. I think I really ought to lance that, and then I'll give it a shot of heteromycin; that's the latest thing for staphylococci like this.'

I couldn't bear to watch, but Richard was absorbing every detail from a range of about six inches. It was a wonder the vet could see what he was doing at all.

'One pound fifty please Mrs Garth. I don't send accounts like Mr Pleasance because it's too much clerical work. Next patient please.'

*　　*　　*

Goldie's paw healed very rapidly and when Mr Bradwell called to see her three days later the inflammation had gone completely.

'Yes that's coming on very nicely. I'll just bathe it and

put a new dressing on, then she should have no more trouble. There Goldie, how's that?'

'It's very kind of you to call,' I said. 'I didn't realize she needed a new dressing. She seems grateful for the attention though. How much do we owe you for that, Mr Bradwell?'

'Oh I can't charge for that. To be honest it didn't really need another dressing but I like to see how my patients are responding to their treatment, and she's a beautiful little bitch.'

'Would you like a cup of coffee while you're here?'

'No I mustn't bother you.'

'I've just made some.'

'Well in that case I'd love a cup.'

Mr Bradwell sat in the large arm-chair, drank three cups of coffee, ate five chocolate biscuits, and told us the story of his life.

'I can't remember ever wanting to be anything except a vet, but that practice in Glasgow nearly put me off for good. Of course I wasn't a partner so I didn't have any say in running things. It was a bit different from Kendal where I come from I can tell you. Anyway I've got my own practice now and I think I shall like it here. In a country practice you look after working animals instead of pets that tend to be either pampered or neglected. Not that I've got anything against pets have I Goldie?'

She rubbed against his leg, and Richard observed, 'Goldie likes Mr Bradwell.'

'I was lucky to get in here,' he continued, 'because quite a number of people wanted to buy the practice. Old Joe Pleasance was really letting it go too cheaply, but he was very choosy about who could have it. Insisted on interviewing everyone, and I reckon it was a stiffer test than my final exam.' He looked at his watch. 'But I shall have to be going or I'll be late for my evening surgery.'

Reluctantly he pulled himself up from the chair and walked out to his Land-Rover. It was a full week before we saw him again.

'I was just passing on the way back from looking at Mr

85

Jamieson's old sow,' he explained, 'and I thought I'd just look in, and see your patient.'

'Goldie's in great shape again now. You'd never guess that she was in such a bad way only ten days ago. Richard. Call Goldie to come and see her visitor. Would you like some coffee Mr Bradwell?'

'Yes please. I can't refuse that.'

Mr Bradwell drank another three cups of coffee, ate three slices of walnut layer cake, and told us all about the life of a country vet.

'And what are you going to be when you grow up young man?' he asked Richard. 'Would you like to be a vet?'

Richard didn't answer. You could hardly expect a child of his age to answer that. Mr Bradwell gave me a strange searching look as if there was something about me he didn't know. 'But I expect you want to be an astronaut. Everybody round here seems to want that.'

'Goldie better now,' Richard informed him.

'Oh yes I'd better have a look at that paw hadn't I?' Stroking the puppy's head with one hand he carefully examined the paw.

'There's not very much wrong with that now is there? I'm afraid I shan't have any more excuse to come and sample your mistress's cakes and coffee.' He looked at me cheekily.

'Richard and I will always be pleased to see you if you are passing and care to stop for a cup of coffee,' I told him.

'Will you? Right then we'll make it next Wednesday.'

He laughed at my surprise then looked thoughtful again.

'No we won't. You've been feeding me so it's my turn to feed you. I'll pick you up after my evening surgery and we'll drive out to "The Swan" for dinner. Can you get a baby-sitter all right? It'll be a bit late for Richard but we'll bring him back a bar of chocolate.'

*   *   *

Dinner at 'The Swan' after evening surgery on Wednesday turned out to be a weekly event and for me it soon became a very important one. Laura used to come and look after Richard, or if she wasn't free old Mrs McGregor would.

George was just as keen on his job as Andrew had been on metallurgy but he talked about it a lot more and of course it was easier for me to understand than Andrew's space research. Although he told me all about himself I didn't say much about myself, not about the last seven years at any rate. He seemed to know all about me all the same, in fact I often got the impression he knew some things I didn't.

'Well I get around seeing everybody in my job, Helen, and they all like to have a chat about local gossip.'

George's hobby was singing and almost the first thing he had done on coming to Bannockside was to get himself enlisted in the local church choir. He persuaded me to go and hear them and I was quite impressed, especially with his strong baritone voice.

He lived alone in a large oldish house that went with the veterinary practice and although a woman came in three times a week to do the cleaning George did all his own cooking. Richard and I used to go there for Sunday lunch and George cooked it all himself. He wouldn't even let me peel a potato. On Saturdays he used to visit us at the cottage.

So you can see we were very good friends, but it wasn't a thing of fire and passion, at least as far as I was concerned. Poor George found me rather unresponsive I'm afraid, but although I knew I should never feel about him quite the way I had about Andrew I very soon reached the point where I couldn't imagine life without him. A dozen times I thought he was going to ask me to marry him but he never did, so I had to.

'George my love. Have you ever thought of asking me to marry you?'

'I think of it all the time Helen, but I can't can I?'

'You can't? Why not?'

'Because you are a wealthy woman and I am teetering

on the edge of bankruptcy and always shall be as far as I can see from the look of this practice.'

'That doesn't stop you marrying me.'

'I didn't say it did, but it stops me asking you.'

'So you have been trifling with my affections all this time.'

'I suppose you could call it that,' he laughed wryly, 'but my own affections are pretty heavily involved you know.'

'I know they are darling, and I'll tell you what we'll do. I will ask you. My money can't be any impediment to that can it? So George Bradwell will you marry me?'

'In answer to the first question, no it can't, and before you change your mind about the second question, yes, yes, yes please.'

We clung together wordlessly. George was the first to speak.

'Helen darling,' he began diffidently, 'I think we should make it just for five years to begin with, don't you?'

I felt as though he had struck me a blow in the face. At that time, you remember, it was only two years after the Matrimonial Reform Acts, which provided for marriage contracts of five, ten, twenty years or life. Nowadays it would be considered an insult to ask someone to marry you for a limited period but in many ways we're more old-fashioned now, aren't we? Certainly five-year contracts were very popular in those days, but it wasn't my idea of married love.

'If you feel that you'll be tired of me after five years I don't think we'll bother.' I pushed him away from me.

'Helen darling, don't take it like that. I love you with all my heart and I am absolutely certain that I shall continue to do so as long as I live. I would gladly bind myself to you for life, but I don't think you should commit yourself so irrevocably.'

'But why George? You know that I love you.'

'I know sweetheart, but I really am only an imperfect substitute for your first husband, and when we are married I shall only have second place in your heart, after Richard. I know and I accept it.'

'I'm sorry George. I really am. I know I'm not fair to you but I can't make myself feel any different. I do love you though.'

'Marry me for five years and I promise you that if you wish we will renew it for another five and another and another as long as we live.'

'It wouldn't be fair to have children,' I warned him. At that time it was actually permissible in a limited-contract marriage; it was about 1990 they made it illegal wasn't it? I wasn't really bothered about having any more because Richard filled my whole life – perhaps it was the effect of all the Population Ministry's propaganda for one-child families – but I assumed that George would want one of his own.

'Yes I know Helen. I've thought about that but I think we should leave it for the five years and if we decide we do want a child we could take out a longer contract then.'

So we left it like that. We were married in the school holidays, in the village church, which was one that recognized limited-term marriages – most churches didn't for a good many years you remember. We had a very small reception with only about a dozen guests. Dr Sanders wasn't one of them but he sent a very handsome crystal vibration clock as a wedding present and he offered his congratulations when he saw me in the village after we got back from the honeymoon.

'Mrs Bradwell. I was so pleased to hear that you had married again and I'm sure you and your husband will be very happy. I do think you were sensible to decide on a five-year contract though. One never knows what the future holds, and in your circumstances a more permanent arrangement might have been unwise.'

Chapter ten

RICHARD AND I moved into George's house, but I decided
to let the cottage rather than selling it. I took most of my
furniture with me and we put some of George's things we
didn't want in the cottage so we could let it furnished. I
didn't know how easy it would be to find a tenant but Mr
Baron said the Space Agency would welcome the use of it
for temporary staff, so we let them have it. Running
George's house was a lot more work than the cottage had
been, to say nothing of looking after George, so I decided
I'd have to give up my job. It was a great wrench though
because I really did enjoy teaching, and besides there was
something else. I was still fascinated by the mystery of the
orphans from the Evercare Home and I felt that it was at
the Bannockside school that their story would unfold.
Richard was growing into a fine healthy boy. There was
no problem about him on his own; it was over the
children as a whole the mystery lay.

'Yes Mrs Bradwell. I quite understand,' Mr Campbell
assured me. 'Of course ye won't be able to look after your
husband and your son and teach full-time. We shall be
very sorry to lose ye though.'

'I shall be sorry to go.'

'Of course if ye'd like to teach part-time I should be
verra happy to arrange it.'

'Could you? You mean I could teach just two days
a week or something like that?'

'That's the sort of thing. Many schools have one or two
part-time teachers. Ye wouldn't have a class of your own
so ye'd mainly be filling in for the others, but ye'd be verra
useful to us. Would ye like me to put in a request?'

'Yes I would Mr Campbell. I'd love to be able to carry
on part-time.'

I was delighted at the prospect. I should be able to keep

in touch with the children and, not having a class of my own, I should be teaching all of them at one time or another. It was arranged that I should work Mondays and Tuesdays, then I had the rest of the week for my household duties.

* * *

The children from the orphanage fascinated me and at that time I had no idea why it was, except that I had adopted Richard of course. There were sixty of them at the school altogether now, thirty boys and thirty girls, and their ages spread over about three years. At first glance you couldn't tell them from the other children but when you got to know them you realized that they were different in some way; they had much more fellow-feeling about one another for one thing. The boys were extremely intelligent, the girls were about average, and they all had a flair for games that was almost uncanny, not individual games – in running, jumping and so on they were not outstanding at all – but in team games.

'All line up now,' I told the girls from Form I. 'I'm taking you for netball today because Miss Jensen is away. Now the first thing is to pick the teams. Who shall I have for the two captains?'

'Molly,' shouted half the girls.

'Alice,' called out the rest.

'Right then. Molly and Alice it shall be. I'll toss a penny to see who picks first.'

Molly and Alice didn't have any hesitation about whom to choose for their teams. Just as I knew they would Molly picked six other girls from the Evercare and Alice chose six from the village. It used to worry me at first that the local children didn't accept the orphans but it wasn't really that. They all got on very well together and it was actually the Evercare girls who insisted on being in the same team.

And of course I knew who would win. It wasn't that the girls in Molly's team could run faster or throw harder or straighter; individually Alice's team were at least as good, but it was the passing and the playing together. Molly's team moved down the yard as if they were joined by invisible threads. When a girl wanted to pass the ball another one was standing ready to catch it, and they didn't even seem to look at one another. At eight-nil I decided it was time for a change.

'Right then we'll mix you up a bit. We'll have two new captains and I'll pick the teams.'

I made sure that the girls were thoroughly mixed up, and we started again, but I'm afraid you could only describe it as no-contest. The village girls played normally, but the others just stood around bewildered. When one of them had the ball as likely as not she would give it to one of the other team, and in the end the Evercare girls just drifted to the side and left the local girls to finish the game.

Roger Limpet said it was just the same when he tried to get the boys playing football.

'I always insist that they mix up,' he told me, 'but it doesn't do a bit of good. Do you know last week Peter McLellan had to take a penalty kick and Donald Beatty was in goal on the other side? Peter was obviously uncomfortable and you could see he didn't want to take the shot but didn't like to refuse. In the end he just gave the ball a gentle tap straight towards Donald's hands.'

'So he didn't score?'

'He did, because Donald stepped to one side and let the ball roll into the net.'

'I suppose they're both . . .'

'Oh yes they both belong to the clan all right.'

'Is that what you call it?'

'For want of a better name, yes, but they're a darned sight more closely knit than that suggests. It beats me. If I let Peter and Donald play in the same team along with the rest of their mates they'd be absolutely unstoppable.'

*   *   *

It took a bit of getting used to the fact that when I

asked a question in class about ten hands were liable to go up simultaneously to answer it, and if I gave them a test you could depend on having them all in a dead-heat. If it were Science the boys of the clan would all be equal top, but in English they might be tying for bottom place. Wherever they were they'd be level. But the boys didn't tie with the girls; in Maths, say, the Evercare boys would all be near the top and the girls near the bottom. It was uncanny, but what really shook me was Miss Travers' discovery.

'Have you ever heard of E.S.P., Helen?'

'Extrasensory Perception,' I said. 'There was quite a bit of interest in it in the nineteen sixties, but I think eventually they decided there was nothing to it, didn't they?'

'I don't know what they decided. I certainly didn't believe in it, but I'm not so sure now.'

'Why? What's happened?'

'It's that memory game we play. What's it called? Kim's game. Someone arranges twenty small objects on a tray and the rest of the class look at them for a certain time, then the tray is covered by a cloth and everybody has to remember the twenty things and write them down.'

'Oh they'd be very good at that. There are some very sharp kids in your class.'

'Ah but you haven't heard it yet. It was Fay Grimes' turn to arrange the tray and, as well as the usual school things like pencils, rulers, and rubbers, she brought some things from home specially. I remember she had one of her father's cufflinks, the knob off an old wireless set, a pickled onion, a chess piece, all totally unrelated.'

'And did the children get them all right?'

'The other girls from the Home did, but that was only to be expected. It was Joan Blake that shook me. She wasn't even there.'

'What do you mean?'

'Joan was the monitor that week, and at the beginning of the lesson I found that the bulb in the slide projector had gone so I sent her to the Head for a new one. Next lesson was Geography so we should need the slides. When she got back Fay had just covered up the tray and the others were writing down what they could remember.'

'Joan couldn't play.'

'That's what I said, but she wanted to try to do it just by guessing.'

'And she guessed them all correct?'

'Yes. Twenty out of twenty, and when I asked her how she did it she couldn't understand what I was on about. Now is that extrasensory perception or isn't it? Your Richard was there. You ask him about it.'

I did when we were at home that evening, and Richard tried to explain it to me.

'It wasn't magic, Helen, and it wasn't a trick. Joan just knew what they would be.'

'But how did she know? Could she see through the cloth?'

'No. Course not. She just thought what things she would have chosen if she had been Fay. So you see she knew what Fay had put.'

'Did you know?'

'Oh no. I only got ten right, but you see Fay's a girl and I'm a boy. If Jack or Malcolm had done them I should have known.'

*   *   *

I haven't told you much about George, have I? We were very happy in a quiet sort of way, and we were very well suited. Perhaps if I had never known Andrew, if George had been my first love, exactly the same magic would have been there. Perhaps at thirty-five one couldn't expect to feel the same deliriously irrational joy one knew at twenty-five. I don't think it was just that though. But we were very happy, and in a way we were better friends than Andrew and I had been. We talked to one another more. George told me all about his practice and what's more I could understand it all. He was very sympathetic about all my trivial household problems and interested in what happened at school. He understood my worries about the orphans.

'They're all right, Helen my love. They're a splendid lot of kids, and our Richard is as bright as any of them.'

'But there's a mystery about them. There's some secret that concerns them all, and where they came from.'

'We don't know who their parents were, but that's the best way with adopted children. They can grow up totally integrated in the family that adopts them.'

'It's not just that though. There's something very special about them and very strange. I think you know something about them that I don't.'

He didn't answer. 'You do, don't you George?' I persisted.

'No,' he said very thoughtfully. 'I don't know anything you don't, but I think I might be able to make a few guesses which you wouldn't.'

'It's the way they're all so close to one another. Roger Limpet calls them The Clan you know.'

'Well he's probably nearer than he thinks. My guess is that they're a clone like the dogs.'

'A clone? What's that?' It sounded something horribly unnatural.

'A group of plants, or animals, or in this case people, all grown from a single parent organism.'

'I don't know what you mean.'

'It's like taking a cutting of a plant, a rose-tree say, or a blackcurrant-bush.'

'You can't take cuttings of people.'

'Theoretically you can. It would require tremendously sophisticated techniques though. But it was tried with Drosophila, fruit flies to you, about five years ago, and last year workers in Melbourne claimed to have done it successfully with mice. So if my guess is right there's somebody around here who's a few years ahead of the Australians. Somebody who hasn't bothered to publish his results.'

The full impact hadn't hit me yet. At present I was

95

merely baffled. 'You mean they can cut a little bit off a mouse and it grows up into another mouse?'

'That's more or less it, but of course there's a lot more to it than that. In fact you've only got to take one single cell but it must be the right kind of cell and it must be kept in the correct environment so that it divides, differentiates, and grows up into the complete organism.'

'Where does it happen? All in a test-tube?'

'The first few weeks might be in something like a test-tube but eventually it would have to be transferred to a full-scale artificial womb or perhaps a substitute mother. But that sort of thing is commonplace nowadays. Half the lambs born round here are not conceived by the ewes that carry them.'

'I can't believe it. It's like Frankenstein and his monster. What were these monster mice like?'

'They were just perfectly normal mice. The only thing was they were all exactly the same, like identical twins. In the case of the mice there were a hundred so I suppose you might call them centuplets.'

'And do you think that Mr Teale's dogs are, what do you call it, a clone?' My mind was still suppressing the real question.

'I don't think there can be any doubt of that. They really are identical, and you notice they're all bitches. They'd have to be all the same sex, that of their single parent.'

'Then the Evercare children aren't one of your horrible clones. Some are boys and some are girls.'

'Oh they're not one clone. There are two clones there. That's quite obvious.'

'And they're not all the same like the dogs. They've got different colour hair for one thing, and their eyes are different for another.'

'Yes I know and I must admit that threw me off the scent for quite a while. There's no doubt somebody's been very very clever about that.'

'What do you mean?'

'I don't exactly know. What you'd call genetic engineering I suppose. They must have found a way of causing random mutations in the hair and eye colour genes without affecting anything else. The genes for hair colour and eye colour are known to be on the same chromosome so it's theoretically possible.'

'It's horrible,' I wept. 'I don't know how you can talk like that, sitting there and making out that our Richard is some kind of a Frankenstein monster.'

'No Helen.'

'Yes you are. You're a callous brute.' For a moment all my shocked horror appeared as hatred of poor George for crystallizing my half-conscious fears and telling me just what I hadn't wanted to hear.

'I'm sorry Helen, but don't be upset. It doesn't really make any difference to Richard.'

'Of course it does. It may not matter to you but it matters to me. How can people be allowed to do such horrible things?' ·

'I'm sure it will eventually have to be made illegal. As a matter of fact there's a private member's bill coming up in Parliament next month making cloning in animals illegal.'

'Animals? Why aren't they more interested in people?'

'I suppose the M.P.s haven't got round to considering that human cloning might be a feasible proposition in the immediate future. Most of the articles I've read seem to concentrate on the possibility of cloning race-horses and I must admit the idea of somebody making a couple of dozen carbon-copies of the Derby winner does cause the mind to boggle slightly. It could be very useful in farming though, for things like beef production.'

'Beef production. That's all you're interested in isn't it? Farmyard animals. You even despise pets because they don't give wool, or milk, or beef, or eggs. Oh I can't stand talking to you any longer.'

I jumped up, rushed out of the room, and ran upstairs. Gently I opened the door of Richard's room and looked at the sleeping figure. I couldn't have loved him more if he'd been my own son, and now they wanted to make out he was some kind of a freak. I must have stood looking at him for ages before I felt George's hand on my shoulder.

'He's a lovely boy, Helen, and he's going to grow up to be a fine man. Please don't worry about anything. Let's go to bed now. I'm sure it won't seem so bad in the morning.'

*   *   *

George's explanation about cloning had answered some questions but it had posed a lot more and after he had dropped off to sleep I lay awake, my mind filled with an endless kaleidoscope of tangled ideas and speculations. If George's ideas were right – I couldn't believe them, I wouldn't believe them – but if they were true who was responsible for such a diabolical scheme? It must be Dr Sanders: It must have all originated at the Space Station. Perhaps it wasn't a space station at all. Perhaps it was a secret biological research station and the space thing was just a cover for all sorts of unimaginable experiments in human physiology. But as my mind roamed over even wilder and wilder speculations it all became more and more unreal until my waking fantasies merged into my sleeping nightmares.

All next day I thought about it, wondering what to do, and by tea-time I still hadn't decided.

'Would you like me to write to Alan Sidcup?' George asked.

'Who's that?'

'He's the man who did the work on fruit-flies. I know him slightly, he's at Cambridge now, and I could write to ask him about the current position of cloning in mammals and possibly humans.'

'You'd better not say anything about the Space Station.'

'No there's no need to do that. As a vet it's quite natural for me to be interested. I'll just write and ask him what the present state of knowledge is.'

George posted the letter that evening, and three days later it came back marked 'Undelivered. Returned to

98

sender'. It wasn't returned by the postman though; Dr Sanders brought it.

'Good afternoon Mrs Bradwell. Is your husband in? No I expect he's out on his rounds. Never mind. It's just that the postmaster asked me to bring this letter back. It couldn't be delivered.'

I assumed that Dr Sanders did not have a part-time job with the Post Office so he'd evidently got something to say about the letter.

'Come in Dr Sanders. Would you like a cup of coffee?'

'Thank you. That would be very nice.'

'Is all the mail from Bannockside being censored now then?' I enquired as I handed him his drink.

'Oh no. That would be a gross infringement of personal liberty, wouldn't it?'

'Only my letters, and my husband's?'

'No of course not Mrs Bradwell, but naturally where vital aspects of national interest are involved we do have to be rather careful.'

'What was wrong with that letter? It's just an ordinary letter. Why was it singled out for your attention?'

'Because it was addressed to Dr Sidcup. I'm sorry it had to be opened but as you see it was done very carefully. You can hardly tell can you? The contents were found to be related to a rather sensitive area of policy which the Home Secretary feels could become the subject of a hysterical outcry if the news media became aware of it at too early a stage.'

I have to admit that for the moment I was at a loss for a reply, but Dr Sanders continued.

'Mrs Bradwell, I know that you and your husband are both intelligent and sensible people, and young Richard is a splendid boy. By the way if for some reason you have any doubt that he is a perfectly normal and healthy child please put it completely out of your mind. He must be the source of great happiness to you both, and I am sure you would not wish to do anything to jeopardize his future. You unfortunately already know much more about certain things than is good for you and I must tell you that any

99

further attempt to pry into matters which should not concern you might have very undesirable consequences. You will recall that I am still the legal guardian of all the children from the Evercare Home.'

I GRADUALLY became reconciled to the idea of Richard's strange origin and accepted the fact that, by whatever bizarre process his life had started, now he was a perfectly normal, healthy, happy, lovable boy. I found it hard to forgive George for telling me about it though. He only told me because I asked him, and then as gently as he could, but unfairly, irrationally I blamed him for the pain his words had caused me.

Poor George. He deserved a better wife, but I did try. He was always gentle and affectionate and I tried to respond. When I'd given up hope of that I tried to pretend, but I knew I wasn't convincing.

And George was a good husband. He gave me everything I asked for and he treated Richard just like his own son. We didn't see much of one another because George would spend his evenings a hundred yards down the road, in the Red Lion, playing darts or talking to the local farmers. He never came home drunk and, although he was sometimes surly and bad-tempered, that was the only thing I could complain of. On Saturdays and Sundays he'd be out all day playing golf, but it didn't bother me because my life was completely centred on Richard.

For his seventh birthday Richard wanted a hovercart. Hovercraft had been in use commercially for years, but the children's version had only just come out and the video ads were full of them. At nine hundred pounds a time not many people had them but I didn't see why Richard shouldn't, since I could afford it. George didn't think much of the idea though.

'In the first place he isn't old enough, in the second place it's a criminal waste of money, and in the third place I don't think they're safe anyway.'

'But they only go about six inches off the ground and he'd only be using it in the garden. I don't see how he could come to any harm.'

'They've got a three fifty c.c. engine, which would be powerful enough to drive a motor-bike at a hundred miles an hour.'

'But hovercarts don't go very fast. The top speed is only twenty-five and the man on the video is always saying how safe they are.'

'I know. And my theory is that if they really were safe he wouldn't need to say it so often. Why don't you let him wait a year or two and then I'll look out for a nice little pony for him?'

'Because this is 1987,' I told him, 'not 1887. You may be still back in the age of horses and carts, but I'm not. You've got to move with the times, you know.'

'Yes I've heard about that, but it may interest you to know that there are more horses in the country now than there have been for the last fifty years. And it may also interest you to know that there'll be a lot more still in the future. It's only a matter of time before petrol engines are banned altogether for private use and children's hover-carts are going to look pretty sick then.'

'They'll drive them by electricity like they're going to cars.'

'I don't think they will, because the power consumption's too high. Still don't take any notice of me. You just go ahead.'

'I think I will. Please don't be offended George, but he's such a good boy and it seems a shame for him not to have one when he's set his heart on it.'

There were several models on the market, and Richard and I decided on the 'Kiddihover' which was about in the middle of the price range. We got it from Fleming's in Aberlochie. I couldn't get it in my car and I didn't want to ask George to fetch it but the salesman said they would deliver it.

I don't suppose you remember what those hovercarts were like because the craze for them only lasted a few years and, as George predicted, the total ban on the private use of petrol engines killed them stone dead. But in the nineteen eighties they were all the rage. The adult two-seater road version didn't make much of an impact; the top speed of 35 m.p.h. was against it and at five miles per gallon it wasn't worth using one on the road where a car could go just as well. They were very popular for use in rough country though and in places like golf-courses. And of course when the miniature model came out for children every boy wanted one.

Richard's arrived on Saturday morning. The two men carried it out of their little van and set it down on the path at the back of the house like a large blue and silver tea-tray with a small seat at one end and the engine at the other.

'Mr Fleming said he'd put a gallon of petrol in for ye,' the driver informed me. 'That'll last ye about an hour and a half. Tell the little laddie to be careful with the skirt. If he gets it torn it'll never get off the ground.'

'It may want the seat adjusting,' the other added. 'His legs are a wee bit short to reach the pedals.'

But the driver was anxious to be away. 'The laddie's father can see to that no doubt. Let us know if ye have any problems. There's a wee book of instructions under the seat.'

Before I really had time to ask for a demonstration or anything they had gone, so Richard and I had to fathom out how it worked. Richard had a remarkable mechanical aptitude and wasn't far off managing on his own, but I wasn't really much help at all. Anyway we succeeded in getting the seat adjusted and Richard sat at the controls.

'Helen. Helen.' George came running out of the house. 'You're never going to let him drive it without any proper lessons or anything?'

'It's supposed to be very simple to drive. The man on the video says you can just sit in and drive off without any instruction.'

'Since most of what you hear on the video is lies that should have put you on your guard for a start. Here Richard. Let me show you how it works.'

'I didn't think you were going to have anything to do with it. I didn't think you liked hovercarts.'

103

'I don't, and I did everything I could to persuade you not to get one, but now you have I'd better try and teach the lad to manage it as safely as possible.'

George had always been very good with Richard and he went to a lot of trouble showing him how to drive his new machine round and round the garden and warning him about possible dangers.

'Remember, Richard, you must not go out of the garden. When it needs petrol I'll fill it up out of a can. And you must remember to keep on the level. Do you understand? If you try to go down the steps it'll crash and you'll get hurt.'

'I'll keep an eye on him George,' I promised. 'He'll only be using it when I'm here.'

It was amazing how skilfully Richard managed the hovercart. Every day when he got home from school he would go straight out to the shed where it was kept, start the engine and glide out on the lawn. Since the kitchen window faced out on the garden I could keep an eye on him while I was seeing to the evening meal. One day I saw that he had set a row of canes on the grass.

'What are they for, Richard?' I asked him.

'It's a test, Helen. I must go through all the spaces and not touch a stick. Like Buck Jackson,' he explained.

Buck Jackson was the character in the 'Kiddihover' ads. Richard swung his cart through the improvised slalom with not a scrap less confidence and verve than the video stunt man. George had been quite wrong to suppose that he wasn't old enough.

I thought at first that the Kiddihover was rather noisy, but after a week or so I got quite used to having the sound accompany my cooking preparations. In fact it was quite soothing, psychologically. I suppose the steady buzzing was an indication that Richard was all right. So when the noise suddenly changed to a high-pitched whine I knew at once that something was wrong.

Without even a glance through the window I raced out of the back door and across the lawn. The hovercart was upside-down beside the rockery, and trapped underneath it was the still figure of my adopted son.

'Richard. Richard. Are you all right?' I shouted, tearing at the roaring metal with futile desperation. 'Richard. Richard. Are you alive?'

'Take it off Helen,' he screamed. 'Take it off me. I can't get up and it hurts my arm.'

The anguish at hearing his cries of pain mingled with indescribable relief at knowing he was alive. Frantically I clawed and heaved at the two hundred pounds of metal and rubber which still vibrated with the racing motor. I couldn't move it. I must run for help. But I couldn't leave Richard like that.

'Help,' I shouted. 'Help. Somebody help.'

Suddenly the roaring vibration ceased and I saw George beside me, his hand reaching under the machine to the ignition key.

'All right Richard. We'll have you out in a couple of ticks. Help me pull this end up, Helen.'

Carefully George carried the whimpering boy into the house, gently laid him on the settee, and partly covered him with a coat.

'There. That's better isn't it? It was a nasty shock though and I think we'd better get the doctor to come and look at you.'

'My arm still hurts ever so much and I can't move it at all.'

George looked at the arm and Richard winced as he touched it.

'It's broken, isn't it?' I said, and Richard cried out in terror.

'I'm afraid it is broken,' George admitted, 'but don't worry, Richard. Doctors are very good at mending broken arms and legs nowadays, much cleverer than us vets.'

*   *   *

The broken arm healed uneventfully and after the hovercart had been repaired I sold it back to Fleming's at a loss of two hundred and fifty pounds. Apparently Richard had been trying to drive it over the rockery, a manoeuvre slightly beyond its capabilities. George was quite right about them not being safe. He never said, 'I told you so,' but I knew he was entitled to, and I resented that fact. I received more explicit criticism from another quarter – in a letter from Dr Sanders.

'Dear Mrs Bradwell, I was very distressed to hear about the accident to your adopted son and I hope he will make a speedy recovery from his injury. You will not mind my pointing out that allowing such a young child to be in charge of a motorized vehicle even although only on private property was at best a serious error of judgement, and might be regarded by some as an act of wanton carelessness. I trust that in future you will discharge your responsibilities rather more conscientiously.'

It was so unjust because everyone knew how carefully I looked after Richard. I worried terribly about anything that was wrong with him. Like the little cough he used to get on his chest in the winter.

'I'm sure his bedroom's damp you know,' I told George.

'We'll move him into the front room if you like.'

'No. That's too small, and it's just as damp. I think the whole house is damp. It's with being on such low-lying ground.'

'I'll get the builder to come and have a look at the damp-course. It seems all right though.'

'Why can't we have a new house? It's just a waste spending money on this one. It's so old.'

'I don't think there are any other houses round here that would be suitable. There's the practice you see. I must have a large ground-floor area for the surgery.'

'You could have the surgery separate from the house, or we could have a new one built. That would be the best thing; we could have everything exactly as we wanted.'

'The only problem is the money. The practice is only just about making money now. If I load it with any more overheads the profits will be negative.'

'That's what an accountant would say, but if you listened to accountants you'd believe that nobody ever made a profit.'

Poor George. I wish I hadn't treated him so badly. I don't know why I was so unreasonable, except that I was so wrapped up with Richard that I couldn't think about anyone else's welfare. After I'd nagged him about it almost continuously for three or four months George agreed that we could have a new house built, and within a year of his giving in we were ready to move.

The new house was about a mile and a half from the old one, further up the hill, not quite so convenient for the veterinary practice, but in a much more healthy situation. It had everything you could wish for, Carnot cycle heating and air-conditioning, a rotating sun-lounge, and a fully electronic kitchen. It also had a very large mortgage.

We were further from the Red Lion now but it didn't stop George spending all his evenings there. What annoyed me most about that was the fact that while he was out of the house he expected me to act as secretary and telephonist, taking messages from the owners of various broken down old farm animals who wanted a vet to rush round and snatch their stock from death's door. I had a message pad beside the telephone – it wasn't one of the latest recording autophones because George said they were too expensive – and when one of his customers rang up I just wrote down what they said, for him to see when he came in and usually to attend to the next day.

The reason I didn't write down the message from Colonel Cavendish's groom was that the pencil was broken and the wretched man was too impatient to wait while I got another one. In any case he didn't want to leave a message for George to attend to the next day; Colonel Cavendish wanted a vet round there to look at his stallion within the hour. I tried to telephone the Red Lion twice but the line was engaged and then the third time it seemed to be out of order so I gave up the unequal struggle. If we'd been at the old house I could have just run down the road. Then Richard woke up with one of his nightmares.

I was up with Richard for nearly an hour, trying to convince him that there were no such things as gremlins.

'They're horrible little men who hide inside machines and make them go wrong,' he insisted.

'It's just a silly thing that people say,' I assured him.

'They broke Mr McGregor's lawn-mower last week, and yesterday they got in the engine of the baker's van so it wouldn't go at all.'

'It's only pretending.'

'The gremlins will get inside me and I shall break down,' he wailed.

'No, of course they won't because there are no such things. When something has gone wrong and nobody knows what's the matter they pretend it's a gremlin doing it. But it's only pretending. It's only a game.'

'Well why does everybody tell lies? If there are no such things why do people say there are?'

I don't think I really convinced him in the end, but eventually he was too tired to argue any longer and he gradually slipped into sleep.

When George came in all thought of Colonel Cavendish's stallion had gone from my head. I remembered it at breakfast next morning.

'By the way, there was a message about Colonel Cavendish's horse last night.'

'What did they say? Is it all right again?'

'I don't know. They wanted you to go and see it. The man was very impatient. He seemed to expect you to go last night but I couldn't get in touch with you. The Red Lion phone must have been out of order.'

'Oh my God woman! Why didn't you tell me before?'

He pushed his half-eaten eggs and bacon away and rushed out to the garage. Seconds later I heard his car race down the drive and half an hour later he was back.

'George. What's the matter?'

'It's dead. A quarter to twelve last night. They called in another vet from Dunburn and the bloody thing dropped dead as he walked in the door.'

'Well it's nothing to get all upset about. It's only a horse.'

'It was a horse all right, a race-horse, and Colonel

108

Cavendish paid a quarter of a million pounds for it eighteen months ago. It cut its foreleg on an old bit of fence yesterday and they called me to look at it. I gave it the usual tetanus antitoxin and then a shot of Equipen in case of any other infection, but the bloody thing must have had some sensitivity. I could have sworn it was going to be all right though. I gave it some antihistamine and hung around for half an hour. They were going to phone me if it showed any more untoward symptoms.'

'I'm sorry George.'

'I probably couldn't have done anything. It was just one of those things. The problem is to convince Colonel Cavendish. At the moment he's raving like a mad thing. He's going to sue me for every penny I've got – that's not very much is it – he's going to report me for unprofessional conduct, and if he were a younger man he would horse-whip me from here to Glasgow.'

'The College will stand up for you, won't they?'

'I'm hoping it won't come to that. I'm hoping the Colonel will calm down and realize that it wasn't my fault.'

But it did come to that, and the Colonel didn't calm down because he was convinced that it was George's fault. The unprofessional conduct case came up first, before the R.C.V.S. Council, and they found in George's favour.

'Discharged without a stain on your character,' I congratulated him.

'Not exactly. They decided that I wasn't guilty of unprofessional conduct which is some consolation I suppose, but anyone reading the account in the papers is going to be left with a definite impression that I'm not a very good vet. They won't even trust me with their budgerigars now, let alone their race-horses.'

All the same I think it would have been more or less all forgotten in a week or two but then the civil case for damages came up, and that dragged on for months.

'How can he sue you for damages when the R.C.V.S. have already found you didn't do anything wrong?' I asked him.

'I'm afraid it's not as simple as that. The ordinary court can still find me guilty of negligence even though the College Council decided I wasn't guilty of unprofessional conduct.'

'You're insured against that sort of thing though, aren't you?'

'Yes I'm insured. It's only that that makes it worth his while to sue me. The sort of damages I could afford to pay personally wouldn't be worth his while, unless he particularly wants to ruin me.'

'Never mind, George. I'm sure it'll turn out all right. It was my fault more than anybody's, for not passing on the message. Surely they'll see that.'

They did eventually, but I was in the witness-box for about two hours, telling them all about George's drinking habits and about the phone being engaged and then out of order, and about Richard's nightmares and everything. Colonel Cavendish's lawyer painted a terrible picture of George lolling drunkenly in the bar of the Red Lion callously knocking back double whiskies while a few miles away a poor tortured horse, gentle innocent creature that it was, fought a desperate losing battle for life, and eventually succumbed as a result of the reckless indifference of the man who had been entrusted by the Royal College of Veterinary Surgeons with the care of all our faithful dumb friends. But the defence counsel was more than a match for him.

'With the utmost respect, Your Honour, I should like to suggest that if Colonel Cavendish wishes to have a tame vet at his beck and call twenty-four hours a day, seven days a week, fifty-two weeks a year, ready to drop everything at a second's notice and rush to the aid of the Colonel's expensive and pampered pets he should employ one. Preferably he should employ at least three so that they can arrange a reasonable shift system, allowing them a few hours for eating and sleeping, and to spend with their families or in necessary recreation. He would be advised to have each one on a long piece of string, or at least to equip them with personal two-way radio

110

telephones so that he can summon them the instant he requires them.'

In the end the case was dismissed and Colonel Cavendish had to pay the costs. I thought George would be triumphant, but he wasn't.

'It's no good, Helen. It's finished me here. I shall have to sell the practice for what I can get and move to another part of the country.'

'But they decided it wasn't your fault. Doesn't that make any difference?'

'Not much. I shall always be remembered as the man who killed Fireball Ginger. My picture's in all the papers with about ten pictures of the bloody horse. And who reads far enough to find out what the court decided? We shall have to leave Bannockside.'

'Where are you thinking of going to?'

'As far from here as I can get. How about Penzance? I wonder if I could find a practice in Cornwall. The trouble is I don't think I shall get enough for this one to buy another. It might be best if I tried to get a job somewhere.'

'George. I couldn't bear to leave here. I couldn't bear it. Please try and keep the practice on.'

George did try. He tried very hard, but it wasn't any use. All the farmers who used to be his customers made excuses to go to someone else. He just had to sit around the house all day, and he sat around all evening too.

'Why don't you go out for a drink?' I suggested. 'Let me come too. You buy me a gin and tonic.'

'I can't, Helen. I've been in the Red Lion once since it happened, and that was enough. All the farmers who've changed over to another vet are too embarrassed to speak to me, and the ones that do speak are so full of insincere sympathy it makes me sick.'

'They'll soon forget all about it,' I reassured him, but I knew they wouldn't just as well as George did, and after another two months George sold the practice and started looking for a job, without a great deal of success at first. But at last something turned up.

'They've accepted me, Helen,' he said when the letter

111

came from the Ministry of Agriculture and Fisheries. 'I'm going to be a civil servant. It'll be a big change, though I don't think I'll be behind a desk all day long. I shall get out a bit, but London'll be a lot different from Bannockside.'

My heart sank. The moment I had been dreading had come, and the question I had wrestled with every night for three months now had to be answered.

'George. I can't come with you. I can't leave Bannockside.'

George didn't speak. I think he had known what was coming. He just looked at me resignedly and I hated myself more than I have ever done. After all that he had been through, with everyone's hand against him, why did I have to be the one to deal the final blow? But I had been through it all over and over again, so many times. If George had to leave Scotland and go to London I ought to go with him. But what about Richard? Wouldn't he settle down in London? He could go to school there and be just as happy there. I knew that I was fooling myself. Richard wasn't quite an ordinary boy. I knew they would never allow me to take him away from the rest of the clan, not for any particularly logical reason, but I knew they wouldn't. I knew I ought to put my husband first, but I knew I never could. I wanted to ask him to stay in Bannockside and live on my money if he couldn't get a job, but I knew that would have wounded him more than anything.

'Oh George. I am sorry. I know I ought to go with you and I would do, but . . .'

'Don't worry, Helen. I understand. I wish very much that you could come with me but I have realized all along it would be impossible. Anyway it's only two months to our fifth anniversary so all we have to do is just not renew it. It's lucky we decided on a limited term, isn't it?'

'I am sorry George. I really am. I never dreamt that things were going to turn out like this. I don't believe in limited-term marriages,' I wept.

'You must admit they have their uses though,' he said

112

ruefully.

'Perhaps we could try again in a year or two when things are sorted out a bit. Perhaps we ...' Again I dissolved into tears.

'Perhaps,' said George. 'We'll leave the matter open shall we? And we'll keep in touch.'

* * *

I had toyed with the idea of asking Dr Sanders if I could take Richard to London but before I had managed to pluck up courage I had a letter from him.

'Dear Mrs Bradwell, It has come to my notice that you are planning to leave this district and return to London. I am sure you are aware that this will involve relinquishing your custody of the boy, Richard Garth, and I should be grateful if you would call at my office to discuss the matter. I am very sorry to hear about your husband's difficulties and I should like to wish you both every success in your new life in the South. Yours sincerely, Edwin Sanders.'

I was so mad it almost made me change my mind, go with George, and take Richard with me, but I knew I shouldn't be able to get away with it. And there were Richard's views to be considered.

'Oh no Helen. I shouldn't be able to come to London with you and George. I have to stay here with all my friends. We can't be separated because we're all part of one another.'

'Do you feel like that about the boys and the girls?' I asked him, and he was quite scornful of my ignorance.

'No of course not. Only the boys, not the girls. Except Sally. She is different from all the other girls. I mustn't be separated from Sally.'

DR LOWREY gave me a prescription for happiness pills and this time I accepted; it was the only way I could live with myself. I only took half a tablet at bedtime though instead of the one every eight hours it said on the bottle but it helped me not to feel quite so guilty about the way I had treated George.

George sold the house along with the practice, and he went off to London. Richard and I moved back to the cottage and I was very glad I hadn't sold it. George had offered to let us stay in the house but it wouldn't have been fair because he couldn't very well have sold the practice without it. We parted without a great deal of drama and emotion, but I knew that George was terribly upset. I was too, but for me the dilemma had resolved itself into a simple choice between him and Richard, and there was never any doubt which way I had to decide. I knew I should have gone with George, but I just couldn't. We did agree that if ever circumstances changed and we were both still free we would consider coming together again.

I went back to working full-time at the school, and once again Mr Campbell was very helpful.

'Yes of course Mrs Bradwell. I've been hoping ye'd soon be able to now Richard's a wee bit older although I'm sorry it's happened this way. I'm sure the Education Committee won't make any bones about it; they give me everything I ask for nowadays. I must be the only head-master in Scotland that can say that.'

It was fascinating to watch the clan growing up. The eldest ones were ten now and would soon be leaving the Bannockside Primary to go to the Senior School at Dunburn. The terms 'grammar' and 'comprehensive' had been dropped you remember, after the long and bitter controversy which began in the nineteen seventies. The so-called grading exams had just been introduced and a lot of people said this was an underhand way of bringing back the old 'eleven-plus' but most of them accepted the Ministry's assurance that they were necessary to let the teachers at the new school know each child's strengths and weaknesses.

The grading exams caused a lot of trouble that year. The examiner came about a fortnight after the papers had been sent off and I suppose if Mr Campbell had been at school he would have explained matters. But the Head was away ill and the examiner wouldn't listen to a word anyone else said. He decided to carry out a full enquiry on the spot. He assembled the whole staff in the Head's study after school and told us just what he thought.

'Ladies and gentlemen, this is a verra serious matter, and in all my thirty years' experience I have never known the like of it. It is the most blatant case of cheating and copying that I have ever encountered, and I assure you that the boys involved will be dealt with in the severest possible way.'

'But what is the matter, Mr Nugent?' asked Albert Ramsey, who was now the deputy head.

'What is the matter indeed? You may well ask that question, and it is a question I myself have been asking. What is the matter with the moral instruction in a school where the children have so little honesty and decency that they will engage in wholesale cheating and copying in an important examination like this? And what is wrong with the staff in a school where the examinations are conducted in a manner which allows such disgraceful events to occur?'

'I'm sure our children wouldn't cheat in an exam,' said Miss Travers.

'All the exams were most carefully supervised,' Mr Ramsay insisted, 'and the papers were kept locked in the Headmaster's safe.'

'That is something I find very difficult to believe in view of the fact that no less than ten of the boys submitted absolutely identical answers.'

'Well they would, wouldn't they?' Roger Limpet commented.

'And what does that mean, may I ask?'

'It's the way their minds work, isn't it? The way they all think alike. We get it all the time.'

'What a preposterous suggestion. I've never heard such nonsense in my life.'

'It is true Mr Nugent,' I said. 'We all find the same thing. You can see from the homework mark register.'

But the examiner wasn't listening. 'Mr Ramsay,' he raved, 'are your staff all weak in the head? Do they think I have never marked exam papers before? I am clearly wasting my time here, but I shall make a full report to County Hall and ye will be hearing more of this I warn ye.'

'Mr Nugent. I think there is something you ought to know. Could I have a word with you in private please?'

'Ye may as well if ye wish, but I warn ye I shall not be prevented from doing my duty by any of your snivelling excuses. The rest of ye may go and I will hear what Mr Ramsay has to say about this disgraceful business.'

I was surprised that the Education Committee had sent us an inspector who didn't know about the special features of our children. It was an oversight I suppose but Mr Ramsay succeeded in smoothing matters over. He was in the know of course but I don't know how much he told Mr Nugent.

One thing that puzzled me was why the boys should get into trouble for all having the same answers but not the girls, so I asked Anne Noble.

'Could you tell me something please Anne?'

'Certainly Mrs Bradwell. What is it?'

'How was it that the ten Evercare girls who took the grading exam didn't all get the same mark? You're just as clever as Molly Landsdown but she got twenty marks more than you. How was that?'

'We thought it would be best, Mrs Bradwell,' Anne answered coolly. 'We thought the examiner might not understand about us all being the same so to save any trouble we decided to make sure we all put different answers.'

Personally I was speechless.

'I hope it was all right Mrs Bradwell,' Anne went on, 'and I'm sorry if we caused any trouble but we thought it would be best.'

'You didn't cause any trouble,' I assured her. 'It was the boys who did that. All ten of them got the same marks and apparently their answers were identical.'

'We did warn them about it Mrs Bradwell. We told them they should have done the same as we were doing but they wouldn't. They said it would be dishonest to fiddle the marks like that.'

'What exactly did you do then?'

'We drew lots.'

'You did what?'

'We drew lots. You know. Before the exam we put all our names in a little box and pulled them out one at a time. We agreed that the one whose name came out first would be top, and so on. I was last,' she added with a barely perceptible tinge of regret.

'Didn't you mind Molly coming top when you could have done just as well?'

'Oh no Mrs Bradwell. Molly is like a part of me so I couldn't be envious of Molly, could I?'

'No of course not and I'm very glad to see that you have such a generous attitude. I think you did quite right to do what you did but I don't think I should tell too many people about it. Now off you go and play with your friends.'

Anne went off and I pondered on the devious nature of my sex. The Evercare boys were more intelligent than the girls but the girls were better endowed with that form of low cunning which is so useful in real life. What they had done was exactly what I should have done in the circumstances. Their complete lack of envy for one another was something more alien to the female nature but I could imagine myself feeling just the same.

*   *   *

It was a few weeks after the business of the grading exam that the affair at the tarn occurred. I had just called the register for Form III and Tom Bennet was absent.

'Does anyone know what's the matter with Tom?' I asked, and immediately Rosemary Waterhouse jumped up.

'I must go and look for him,' she said anxiously. 'I must see what's happened to him.' And she rushed out of the door and across the playground.

The rest of the class looked at one another for a few seconds, then nine of the boys ran out to follow her. The other girls from the clan stood up, uncertain what to do, but the rest of the boys and girls were quite unmoved.

'Should we go and help Rosemary,' Jane Dancy asked the others, 'or should we leave it to the boys to find Tom?'

'The boys will find him,' they agreed, and quietly the girls sat down to continue their lesson.

But I was on my way out, in time to see boys streaming from the other class-rooms and a galloping mass charging out of the gate and up the road. I couldn't keep up with them but I was in time to see them turn up Heathercroft Lane, the path Tom should have come down to school. Roger Limpet and Albert Ramsay had joined me now and, puffing somewhat, we half ran half walked up the lane.

'We've lost them I'm afraid,' I panted.

'It doesn't matter,' said Mr Ramsay. 'There's only one way they can go.'

For the next half a mile the going was pretty steep and we soon slowed down to a walk. At the top of the hill the path dropped down again to Wayside Tarn and there was the most incredible sight I have ever seen in my life.

Wayside Tarn has very steep banks at that end. The water level was about twenty feet below the path, the sides sloped about 30° to the vertical, and hanging over the edge of this miniature cliff was a human chain of small boys, each one's arms firmly linked round the waist of the one in front of him. At the top of the chain a group of four boys, with arms linked, secured the others to the stump of an old tree.

'Oh my God! What are they up to?' cried Mr Ramsay as we stumbled down the path to the tarn.

A glimpse over the edge revealed the purpose of the exercise. Tom Bennet lay on a narrow ledge at the water's edge, one leg doubled awkwardly under his body, and beside him knelt Rosemary Waterhouse. The other boys were attempting to drag them to the top.

The men and I watched, terrified of interfering lest the distraction should precipitate disaster, as Tom was lifted slowly and carefully to the top, and gently lowered on to a bed improvised from twenty-nine school blazers.

'We'd better keep him still now and send for an ambulance,' said Mr Ramsay, taking charge. 'It looks as if the poor laddie's broken his leg so it's best not to move him. We maun make sure he's warm though.'

The Deputy-head 'telephoned for help with his pocket radio-communicator, walkie-talkie sets I think we used to call them in those days, and within ten minutes the ambulance was landing on the grass beside the tarn.

*   *   *

Back at the school I gave the boys from my form a good talking to.

'You could very easily all have been killed,' I said. 'You were very brave boys but it would have been best to run and get help you know. The helicopter could have lifted Tom off the ledge directly and that would have been a much safer way of doing it.'

'But Tom was frightened Mrs Bradwell.'

'His leg was hurting him, and he was afraid he would fall in the water.'

'Tom was calling to us to help him, Mrs Bradwell. We had to go to him as soon as we knew he was in danger.'

'Why did you go with the boys Rosemary?' I asked. 'Why did you go and not any of the other girls?'

'I had to go because Tom is my special friend.'

'Aren't you boys and girls all friends with one another?'

119

I asked.

'Yes of course, Mrs Bradwell, but every girl has a boy who is her special friend. Mr Campbell says it was decided when we were born and he says that in a little while we shall be even more special.'

I asked Richard about it when we got home and I knew what his answer would be.

'Yes of course Helen. It's Sally Grantham. Sally and I belong to one another. When we are grown-up we shall be married.'

'Is that so? Have you asked her by the way?'

'Oh no. That would be silly wouldn't it? We're only children. Children don't ask one another to marry them.'

'Well how do you know that you're going to marry Sally? You might decide you like one of the other girls better, or perhaps even somebody you've never met yet.'

'No I couldn't do that.'

'Did Mr Campbell say that you and Sally belonged to each other, or was it Dr Sanders?' I knew that the Director was always likely to be involved in any mystery concerning the children.

'You do say some silly things, Helen. Why should anyone need to tell us that? We can tell that easily enough, can't we?'

I left it at that, and in fact it wasn't until several years later that I got to the bottom of it.

*   *   *

At the end of that year the Director retired. I hadn't realized that he was anywhere near retiring age but from what was said at his farewell party it was clear that he'd reached the statutory fifty-five.

I didn't actually receive an invitation to the reception but Laura asked me to go with her and Tom. They'd been sent two tickets and Laura got Tom to ask for another one, for a friend. Tom and Laura seemed to have patched things up, on the surface at any rate; I was never sure how things really were between them but they behaved as if they were friends again.

I don't think Dr Sanders could have known they were taking me, because when I met him he looked as if he'd seen a ghost. One moment he was chatting happily to Alec and Shirley Teale and then he turned and caught sight of me. The blood drained out of his face as I watched but he didn't lose an atom of his self possession.

'Why this is a pleasant surprise. How kind of you to come and join all my other friends at this last social event in my life at Bannockside.'

'Are you going to leave the district?' I enquired politely.

'Yes I'm leaving Scotland and going back where I came from, the Norfolk Broads. I'm leaving the Space Station in the capable hands of Dr Franks, whom incidentally I don't suppose you have met yet. Let me introduce him to you.'

The blond-haired athletic-looking man beside him stepped forward. 'Good evening Mrs Garth. I'm very pleased to meet you. I've heard so much about you.'

'It's Mrs Bradwell now,' Dr Sanders interrupted, somewhat put out.

'Oh yes of course. Please forgive me. Dr Sanders had told me you'd married again. I understand it was just a limited-term union, quite a popular idea now.'

I decided that I wasn't going to like the new Director any more than I did the old one. And yet his face had a boyish, candid, honest look which made me feel that I could trust him at any rate.

'Are you going to come and hear the choir in a minute? It's a special programme of Dr Sanders' favourite music.'

'I don't think Mrs Bradwell will be interested in that, would you Mrs Bradwell? I'm sure you'd rather stay in the lounge.'

'As a matter of fact I should like to hear the choir. I'm not usually a great one for music, but Richard would never forgive me if I missed it.'

Richard had told me what they were singing and apparently the Director's favourite music was old German lieder. It wasn't my favourite but of course I wanted to hear Richard.

The choir consisted of the thirty boys of the clan and, although I usually regard these old German songs as rather dreary, on this occasion they were enchanting. All the boys were beautiful singers but it wasn't their individual skill that impressed me so much as the way they sang together, the perfect timing, the delicate counterpoint, and the exquisite harmonies. But much as I enjoyed the music something else affected me very much more. The ten eldest boys were on the back row and, as I looked at the line of faces, identical except for hair and eyes, the scene seemed to dissolve in front of me and in place of the ten faces I saw only one, a face familiar to me from an old photograph. Perhaps the Director's half-hearted attempts to put me off seeing the choir had had some point – not much though because I saw them every day in school, so it was only a matter of time before I found out anyway.

*　　*　　*

When I got home from the reception I hunted out Andrew's old tapes. He'd kept records of school concerts and other interesting events from the age of about ten, all neatly dated and catalogued. I never listened to them because it upset me too much; in any case the early ones were all on the old reel-to-reel tape and I hadn't got a machine to play that. But Mr Campbell had an old tape-machine and he willingly lent it to me when I asked him.

One of the earliest tapes was of the Colorado Springs Junior Choir and Andrew had sung a solo. It was 'Heidenröslein'.

Blinded with tears I listened to the pure soaring notes of the boy soprano, of Andrew, of Richard, it could just as well be Leslie, David, John, Malcolm, or any of the boys I had heard singing that same song a few hours before. On the other tapes the young Andrew, Eb they called him then, spoke and sang with an American accent, as Richard and his friends did not. But 'Rose Among the Heather' was in German.

It was confirmation, hardly needed, of the knowledge that had come to me at the concert.

'Did you know who the Evercare boys' father was?' I asked Mr Campbell when I took his tape-machine back. 'I suppose you know that they're a clone, whatever that is.'

'I've never been officially informed,' he told me, 'but I guessed their origin a long time ago and I know enough about developments in biology to understand roughly what it means. I'm terribly sorry that you should be caused so much pain my dear. It was only a few weeks ago that I realized their father was your late husband but I never knew him very well of course. The poor bairns have no mother. I thought it would be easiest for you if you found out for yourself rather than being told. It was only a matter of time, wasn't it?'

'What made you guess it was Andrew Mr Campbell?'

Without replying the Head went to his desk and returned with a long photograph, which I recognized as a black and white version of the latest school photograph. My copy was coloured of course; I hadn't seen a black and white photo for years.

'We had black and white proofs from all the negatives before we decided which one to use,' he explained. 'It was when I saw them that I knew.'

I could see what he meant. On the coloured picture every one of the boys was different; Donald's hair was golden, Peter's light brown, Jack's eyes were blue, Malcolm's greeny grey. In black and white the shades weren't quite identical but some of them weren't far off, and the effect was uncanny. Tears filled my eyes again as I looked at the boys on the back row, at Andrew, and Andrew, and Andrew.

'Oh Mr Campbell,' I wept. 'What shall I do? Whatever shall I do?'

Chapter thirteen

MR CAMPBELL had suggested that I should go and see Dr
Franks, the new director, but I didn't fancy that. I'd had
more than enough of talking to Dr Sanders, and it was
pretty obvious that the new director was cast in roughly
the same mould. Instead I had a talk with Richard. I had
often wanted to talk to him about his strange origin but
I didn't think it would be right. Now he brought up the
subject.

'Please don't be unhappy Helen. I can't bear it when
something makes you upset.'

'It's all right, Richard. I'm not upset.'

'Sally says you are and I expect she's right because girls
know about things like that a lot better than boys do.
Sally says you're very unhappy because my father is dead
and because I haven't got a mother.'

I looked at him helplessly.

'I don't mind not having a mother, honestly Helen. I've
got you and I bet you're just as good as a mother.'

'Do you know who your father was, Richard?' I asked
him.

'I don't know his name but Dr Sanders told me once
that he was very clever and very brave, and he said I'm
just like him.'

My heart warmed slightly towards the old director.
Only slightly though. It really was a great relief to know
that he had retired; the new one couldn't help but be
some improvement.

*   *   *

I got used to the fact that the Evercare boys were all
duplicates of Andrew more easily than I expected to. In
the early nineteen nineties people had become more ra-
tional in many ways. During the whole of the twentieth
century life had been altered out of all recognition by four

great technological revolutions, in engineering, chemistry, then physics, and finally in biology. The first three had all brought their own disasters, they had all given men power they were not equipped to control, but we were ready for the biological revolution, or so we thought in those first few years of the last decade of the century. All over the earth people were better educated. The world was better organized. We were equipped to deal with any problems which the new biological advances would bring, or so we thought in nineteen ninety one, and two, and three.

Admittedly some of the old ideas of freedom had had to go. A lot of things had to be made illegal and a lot of others were compulsory. Critics of the Administration, like the New Liberals, would shout it like a battle-cry. 'Everything is either illegal or compulsory.' The Prime Minister used to say, 'Go on. Shout as much as you want to. The very fact that we allow it shows that you have the freedom you demand.' On their days off from the labour camps and on visiting days at the asylums liberals were allowed to appear on the video to put their views, but nobody took any notice of them of course.

Everywhere men were thinking about the implications of the new medical advances, and what new laws were required to prevent their abuse. The man-child pill was typical. A simple little white tablet to ensure that a woman would have a son – you can imagine the disastrous effect that would have had on world population balance if the Confederation hadn't stepped in with a five thousand percent tax on it. Even then enough slipped through on the black market to cause a lot of trouble until the death-penalty was brought in for smuggling.

You remember all the scandals about the organ pirates, of course. That problem solved itself once cheap reliable mechanical replacements were available but even they would have got out of hand if the Administration hadn't ruled that everyone who was more than fifty per-cent mechanical should have his human rights withdrawn. Without medicare the wretched semirobs, as they were called, died off in months.

The anti-aging pill could lead to a world of ancient pensioners, but it looks as if they're going to make it compulsory to mix in one percent of lethal tablets, doesn't it? And who knows what might have resulted if genetic engineering hadn't been controlled now?

But all these advances, and the government's counter-measures, chiefly had their effect in the big towns. At Bannockside life went on almost unaffected, except that we had the children. Human cloning was made illegal in nineteen ninety two, about fifteen years too late to save me the anguish of my daily encounter with the thirty Andrews. And yet I couldn't regret what had happened. Andrew was dead but I didn't want to forget him so why should I bother about the daily reminders? I had to admit the children brought me a great deal of happiness, especially Richard, my own dear Richard.

*   *   *

When Richard's form, the youngest of the clan, left Bannockside Primary School for Dunburn Senior School I asked for a transfer as well, because I wanted to see them growing up. The Education Committee were quite agreeable; I expect it suited them because now that the number of pupils was down again they couldn't carry the same number of teachers.

'I shall be sorry to see ye go,' Mr Campbell told me, 'but I quite understand your feelings. In any case I shall be retiring meself at the end of the year. Ye'll mebbe find things a wee bit different at the senior school ye ken but I dinna think ye'll have any difficulty with discipline.'

Dunburn was about ten miles from Bannockside and the children went in the school bus. I went by car though because I often needed to get there before they did and I couldn't always guarantee finishing in time to catch the bus. I had changed my car again, this time for an electric two-seater. The Microbe had been showing signs of its age; they were never as reliable as the old Minis, and when the Emmerson-Clive Act was passed I decided to get rid of it. After the anti-pollution and the energy conservation lobbies finally succeeded in their joint campaign to get the internal-combustion engine banned from private cars a period of three years was allowed for the change-over, and during that time the price of second-hand petrol cars slumped steadily down to zero. There was talk of conversion kits but I felt a bit doubtful about how they'd work and I sold the Microbe while I could still get something for it.

You've probably forgotten how primitive electric cars were in the nineteen nineties. For a start the cheapest ones had the old lead accumulator batteries so their range was pitiful and, although they didn't pollute the atmosphere with petrol fumes and carbon monoxide, if they weren't maintained in absolutely perfect condition they tended to leave a strong smell of ozone wherever they went and that was far worse. But my electric two-seater served to get me to school and back on one charging so I didn't complain.

* * *

John M. Tranter, the headmaster of the Dunburn school, was younger than Mr Campbell and his accents revealed that he came from America, from San Francisco, in fact, he informed me.

'Welcome to Dunburn Senior School Mrs Bradwell. You'll find it a bit different from old Jock Campbell's little outfit but I reckon it's not going to take you too long to settle in. I had a letter about you from Jock and he says in his opinion you're a fine teacher. The students are a little older than you've been used to but they're not much trouble and some of them are very very gifted. You know about the brothers and sisters I guess.'

'The clones?'

'That's the scientific term. Thirty boys as like as peas in a pod and the closest buddies you could imagine. And thirty girls that are just the same. But of course your Richard is one of the group. Richard Garth?' He said it with a hint of query in his voice.

'Ebenezer Garth was my first husband,' I explained,

'and after he died I married George Bradwell, but that was just a five-year contract and I'm on my own again now.'

Mr Tranter hesitated for a moment as if uncertain whether to offer his sympathy or not, then he changed the subject.

'There is a thing you'll find strange about the sixty – they're all going steady.'

'Going steady?' I echoed, but I knew what he meant. 'It's natural, isn't it, now they're finding out that boys and girls are different?'

'Vive la différence,' he murmured in a somewhat un-Parisian accent. 'It's natural all right, but they are a bit young and back home when boys start dating girls they reckon to look around a bit, to play the field. These are like old married couples.'

'I've noticed it with Richard and Sally Grantham, but I didn't know they were all like that.'

'The older ones are much worse. You'll come across it if you take them for any subjects that involve pairing at all.'

One of the subjects in my time-table was games, and in the summer the children played tennis. At that time cricket was still popular in the southern counties and in parts of Yorkshire but I don't think they played it in any Scottish schools, certainly not at ours.

I only took the girls and I'm afraid I couldn't give them any expert tennis coaching but I knew the rules and how to do the basic strokes. Phil Saxon, who took the boys, was a very good player and sometimes we swapped over so that he could give the girls the benefit of his expertise while I just watched the boys playing. As at the junior school about half the children in some forms were members of 'the family' as Mr Tranter called it, and when they played against one another we had the old problem of getting them to play hard enough.

'Look Alan,' I said. 'I know that Jack is a friend of yours but you're not going to give him a very good game of tennis just patting it over where he can easily hit it back. It's your serve. Now just see if you can ace him.'

Alan threw the ball up and hurled his racquet at it, with perfect timing resulting as much from luck as from skill. The ball flashed across the net and raised the merest puff of white dust from the corner of the service court before crashing into the back netting. Jack waved his racquet at it helplessly while Alan covered his eyes in anguish.

'I'm sorry Jack. I didn't mean to hit it as hard as that.'

'Good shot,' I told him. 'Now when you can serve like that every time you can call yourself a tennis player.'

'But Jack couldn't get it back.'

'No. And he never will unless he gets a bit of practice at it, will he? If you just give him little patty shots to hit back how is he going to get on when he plays against one of the other boys?'

They saw the force of my argument and both played flat out, but of course the set was a draw at six all. We'd had so many marathon sets that Phil and I had had to make a special local rule that any set which reached six all was a draw.

On the last Wednesday of term Phil and I decided to arrange a mixed tennis drive, and that was where we ran up against the pair-bonding. They chose their partners for the first game and that was all right, but then they had to move around and no one wanted to.

'Couldn't I keep on playing with Anne?' asked Peter.

'Molly and I should like to carry on playing together,' David informed me.

'You stupid children,' I cried in exasperation. 'Haven't I just explained it to you? A tennis drive is like a whist drive. You change partners after every round, to give everyone a fair chance. That's the idea.'

They had to change partners since we insisted but all the time each boy was gazing round at the other courts to see how his own girl-friend was getting on, and when they played against one another it was pathetic. We hadn't sorted that problem out by the end of the afternoon.

And it was just the same at the dancing club.

At the Dunburn Senior School all sorts of out-of-school

activities were encouraged, and each member of the staff was expected to be responsible for at least one. I took the dancing club and all the children of the clones belonged to it. It was inevitable I suppose that either none or all of them should belong.

As you can imagine the boys and girls paired off in their usual way, but after a couple of weeks I decided to put my foot down.

'Listen children,' I said. 'You are supposed to be learning to dance, and I don't take that to mean learning to dance with just one partner. You should be able to dance with any partner, so let's have you mixed up a bit for the next number.'

They did, but you've never seen such shyness. Leslie held Alice in his arms as if she belonged there, but when I made him dance with Rosemary they stood about three feet apart and looked as if they were terrified of touching one another. It was incredible. Rosemary and Alice were like identical twins with only about half a shade of difference in the colour of their hair to distinguish between them. Sometimes I couldn't tell them apart, but Leslie could. One he adored, completely at home in her company, the other filled him with prickly embarrassment.

Every one of the boys could pick out his own girl-friend with his eyes shut at two hundred yards in the dark. Although there was one occasion on which it didn't work. That was at the dancing class and it was the only time I ever saw two of the boys fighting.

We had finished the dancing lesson and the children had gone off two by two as usual. I was just putting my coat on and locking up when Richard and Sally came rushing back in, hand in hand, very agitated.

'Helen. Helen. Come quickly. Jack and David are fighting. They're hurting one another Helen.'

I rushed out to see the two boys standing face to face, raining blows on one another like in one of the old-fashioned boxing matches they used to have when I was a child. As I reached them David fell to the ground, then got up and slunk away, followed by Molly Landsdown, anxiously looking into his bruised face.

'David,' I called out, 'are you all right?'

'Yes I'll be O.K. Mrs Bradwell. I'm sorry I caused so much trouble. I made a mistake.'

Jack remained, guilty and upset, with Jane in solicitous attendance.

'What happened Jack?' I asked him. 'Why were you fighting with David?'

'I didn't want to fight, Mrs Bradwell, but he was trying to take my Jane away. He was holding her arm and he was going to take her home. I said he couldn't but he didn't take any notice. I didn't mean to hurt him Mrs Bradwell. Do you think he'll be all right?'

'Yes Jack. Don't worry. It's just a few bruises. He'll be none the worse,' I assured him.

It was very strange to have two of the Evercare boys fighting, even more strange that it should be over a girl when they were all so devoted to their regular girl-friends. Another unusual feature of the incident was that a contest between two of the boys of the same age should have ended up as anything other than a draw. But that might have been because David was a bit under the weather. I'd noticed earlier in the evening that he had a very nasty cold.

*   *   *

It was just after the incident at the dancing class that I had a little note from Dr Franks asking me if I would call and see him at his office and, curious to know the reason, I telephoned in and fixed a time.

'Good afternoon Mrs Bradwell. I'm sorry to bother you like this but I wondered if you might be able to help me with a little matter.'

'I'd be happy to help you in any way I can.'

'Come and sit down. Let me fetch you a cup of tea. Do you like chocolate biscuits?'

Dr Franks' office was furnished as luxuriously as it had been in Dr Sanders' time but somehow it had a warmer

131

and more friendly atmosphere now. The light no longer shone in a visitor's face and one was not so dominated by the Director's desk and chair.

'I should like to ask you about Dr Garth, your first husband, Mrs Bradwell. I regret very much that I never had the honour of knowing him.'

'What would you like to know, Dr Franks?'

'Nothing much. Just this. Did you have any reason to suspect that Ebenezer did not have perfect eyesight?'

'Of course he didn't. He was as blind as a bat without his glasses.'

'But no one has ever told me that Dr Garth wore glasses. He isn't wearing them in any of the photographs we have. There is nothing in his dossier about it, and I am sure that if his eyes had been weak he would never have been selected. Eyesight was one of the most important things in the original specifications.'

'Andrew, Ebenezer that is, wore contact lenses,' I explained.

It was a few seconds before Dr Franks' gales of laughter subsided and he was able to continue the conversation. 'Dr Garth wore contact lenses. Of course that's the explanation. Why ever didn't I think of it?'

'He never told anyone,' I ventured.

'But my word someone has blundered haven't they? It's lucky for Dr Sanders that he's retired out of the way. Still it's not absolutely fatal I suppose. They can all wear contact lenses if necessary.'

'Are some of the boys short-sighted?' I asked him. 'I've been watching for signs of it in Richard because I knew it was bound to crop up eventually, but he's all right so far.'

'It's just the ten eldest boys at the moment but the others are bound to follow on next year and the year after. There are certainly going to be questions asked in high places. The only excuse, I suppose, is that contact lenses were not so commonplace in the nineteen seventies as they are now.'

'It's not really much of a disability, is it?'

'Not in everyday life, but on the mission conditions are

going to be pretty critical. Success or failure, life or death, may turn on one man's quickness of perception and speed of reaction.'

'What are you talking about, Dr Franks? What mission?'

'The Jupiter Mission of course. I thought you knew what the children were being trained for.'

The Director might as well have struck me a blow between the eyes. I reeled from the shock. 'You mean my Richard and all his friends are going to be the crew of a space-rocket?' But of course. How could I have been so blind? For what other purpose would they have been bred at a space-station?

'I'm sorry to have broken it to you so abruptly Mrs Bradwell but I thought you knew. All the children know. They know it is their destiny and they accept it. None of them would have it otherwise. They are a closely knit group and while they all have one another they are self-sufficient.'

'It's in two thousand and five,' I whispered, still distraught from the shock.

'Let me pour you another cup of tea,' said Dr Franks sympathetically. 'Is there anything else you would like me to explain? Dr Sanders told me you knew all about the project, but if there is anything you want to know I'd be very happy to fill in the details.'

'I don't know,' I stammered. 'I'm all in a muddle. My mind's confused. I can't remember what I do know. Tell me from the beginning.'

'That probably would be best,' he agreed, 'so drink up your tea and have another biscuit and I'll go back to 1975, which is when it officially started. A lot of the planning had been done before, but it was 1975 when the Four Power Space Agreement was signed. Then Russia and China pulled out so it was just America and Europe.'

'Andrew and I came in 1975,' I murmured dreamily.

'Yes I know. You were in it right from the beginning. Anyway, it had been decided that because of the exacting nature of the mission that was planned the crew would need to meet extremely stringent requirements, physically and mentally. Moreover they would have to be capable of working together with a degree of harmony much greater than is usually found in the closest of friends.'

I was beginning to see the logic of it. 'So they decided to breed them specially?'

'Work on cloning in animals, unpublished at that time, had shown that it was possible. The genes of a cell from the human body contain the information required to determine all one's inherited characteristics, and methods had been developed which allowed the cell to multiply, first producing a number of identical cells and then dividing and differentiating to produce perfect human embryos.'

'George told me about that.'

'So they just had to find one suitable man to be the founder of the dynasty. Then thirty replicas could be made. Three hundred thousand men were screened, all without their knowledge.'

'How was that?'

'They were organ-donor volunteers. The Administration had a full medical dossier on every one. They also had biopsy specimens and a written agreement from each one that their tissues could be used for medical and scientific purposes. It was considered that legally this covered the present project. Legally it may have, but personally I think the ethics were rather doubtful.'

'Outrageous might be a more accurate term,' I suggested.

'Anyway, thirty male and thirty female embryos were obtained and grown to maturity in the Station incubators.'

'Why aren't the children all the same age?'

'Because there were only twenty incubators, so they had to keep the other forty embryos in special low-temperature storage until they could be grown up.'

'And they're not quite identical. That's always puzzled me. They have different coloured hair and eyes.'

'Yes,' Dr Franks laughed, 'that was a refinement sug-

134

gested by one of the molecular biologists. A very fancy bit of genetic engineering and I can't pretend to understand exactly how it was done. I know they had to build something called a super-sub-micro-manipulator for it.'

'What about the thirty girls?' I asked.

'Well we couldn't send a crew just of men could we? The Space Agency is not that inhuman. Men and women need one another. Besides, there are many skills for which women are much better adapted than men. A crew of thirty men and thirty women seemed the most logical.'

'I mean did the girls come from the same parent cell as the boys? Did somebody do a clever bit of genetic engineering to change their sex?'

'What a disgusting thought. Good heavens no. The female genotype was selected in the same way as the male, by screening organ-donor volunteers.'

'And was it anyone we know?'

The Director looked at me very hard before he answered. 'That's not very likely is it? With a quarter of a million candidates to choose from it's not very likely that she would also be someone from round here.'

Chapter fourteen

THE JONSON-BALLARD Act was passed in 1996 and its effects were immediate and disastrous.

Tobacco consumption had been declining slowly since 1985 when the multimillionaire Gerard-Slater had sued Atlantic Tobacco for loss of life-expectancy through contracting lung cancer, and had been awarded two million dollars compensation. Legal experts had ruled that the only way the tobacco companies could avoid paying out to everyone who had the disease was to make people buying a packet of cigarettes sign a special form indemnifying the company and its agents. This proved somewhat off-putting but smoking still continued at only a slightly lower level.

The use of alcohol on the other hand had been growing, mainly as a result of a number of technical innovations that had enabled the British wine industry to take over a market previously dominated by France and Germany.

And then there were a lot of miscellaneous drugs used illegally with a wide variety of pharmacological effects, many of them still incompletely understood.

It was to clear up this muddle that the government had appointed the select committee under Sir William Jonson-Ballard to report on the most suitable intoxicant which the British people should be allowed to use. They came down heavily in favour of a total ban on tobacco, alcohol, and all drugs except one. This was THC, tetrahydrocannabinol, and their recommendations were immediately incorporated in the act which bore Sir William's name.

A ban on tobacco and alcohol would have been unenforceable before the 1990 Penal Reforms. You remember how ineffective the old system of fines and prison sentences was, but the 1990 Act abolished these and introduced the two simple measures we have today – tax-code adjustment for first offenders and compulsory crime-aversion therapy for those convicted three times or more. The prospect of paying double income-tax for several years was such a deterrent that aversion therapy, brain-washing as it used to be called, was hardly ever required, except in the case of individuals unable to earn enough money to pay tax on.

So the use of tobacco and alcohol ceased abruptly and the underground THC manufacturers flooded the market with their now legal products.

*   *   *

In 1996 Richard was sixteen and old enough to drive a car of up to five kilowatts. All the children learned to drive at school in the grounds, so when they reached the required age it didn't take much practice on public roads before they were ready to take the test. Like all the boys Richard passed on his second attempt, somewhat mortified to know that the girls had passed first time.

'Can I borrow the car to go and see Sally please Helen?' Richard asked only a few weeks after he'd passed the test.

'Yes all right,' I agreed, 'but make sure you go carefully. You've not had much experience yet you know.'

'Don't worry, Helen. I'll be all right.'

'I shall expect you back by half past ten,' I warned him.

I watched him set off, driving carefully enough, then I went back into the cottage to worry about whether he'd be all right, and every so often I looked out of the front door to see if he was coming back yet. About the fourth time I saw Mrs McLellan, whose adopted son Peter was in Richard's class.

'Mrs Bradwell. Mrs Bradwell. Come quickly. Have you seen what's going on by the loch?'

My eyes followed her pointing finger to a crowd of people about three-quarters of a mile up the road. 'What is it? What's the matter?'

'You'd better come and see. Your Richard's there.'

I rushed after her to the large group of people standing along the fence at the side of the road and pushed into a gap to see what was happening. Some thirty cars had been driven on to the grass at the side of the loch and were lined up as if ready to start a race. I recognized my own among them and began trying to squeeze through the fence to run to it, but before I had got through the cars started up and came charging towards us in a cloud of dust and sparks.

I watched, terrified, as the cars roared past at twice the speed I had thought any of them capable of, their sides crashing together as they jockeyed for position and tried to overtake. Within a minute it was all over and the cars stood smoking and battered at the end of the course, all except for one which had overturned into the water and another whose engine had burnt out halfway down. Boys and girls began to get out of the cars and their elders scrambled over the fence and rushed towards them filled with a mixture of anxiety, fury, and relief.

'What the hell do you think you're playing at?' I demanded as Richard helped Sally out of my car.

'Just a bit of "Hot Sparkers",' he informed me nonchalantly.

'Hot what?'

' "Hot Sparkers". It's all the rage you know. Racing with hotted up cars.'

'What do you mean hotted up? What did you do to my car to make it go as fast as that?'

'Just altered a few connections to shunt out some of the resistance, but don't worry. I'll put them back for you to use tomorrow.'

'You'll put them back this very minute and I'll drive you home my lad, if the armature's not burnt out and the battery's not absolutely flat.'

'You are an old stodge Helen. Try it like it is. It goes like a bomb. Its wheels never even touch the ground.'

Sally giggled. 'Don't take any notice of Richard, Mrs Bradwell. He's stoned out of his mind.'

'He's what?'

'He's stoned. I mean he's a bit fuzzy in the head. I am as well but we'll be all right in the morning.'

'Here. Have you been taking THC?'

'Why not? It's legal isn't it? And I'm old enough now I'm sixteen.'

I drove Richard home; the car would still go although one side needed a respray. Mr Grantham hustled Sally into what remained of his electric superrunabout – it had been loaned to a couple whose parents had more sense than to lend their own car – and angrily drove off in a cloud of blue smoke with a lot more sparks than usual.

Richard was docile and apologetic when I got him home.

'I'm sorry about the car, Helen. I'll try and touch up the scratches, honestly.'

'They're a bit more than scratches I'm afraid. Why did you ever have to behave in such a stupid fashion?'

'It's the stuff I guess, the "Relaxatabs". Haven't you seen them advertised on the video? Pure tetra-hydro. They help you not to worry. Here. Have a couple. They'll help you forget about the car being damaged. They'll help you not to mind.'

'What's the use of that?' I said angrily. 'The car will still be damaged, won't it? You stupid wicked boy. Besides wrecking the car you might have killed someone. You might have killed yourself. You might have killed Sally.'

I think that did get through to him, but he said nothing.

'Now just you get off to bed,' I went on. 'I haven't time to waste talking to you until you've got some sense in your head.'

*   *   *

None of the children ever touched THC again. I think Dr Franks and Alec Teale did a private brain-washing job on them.

But it was going on all over the country, on a smaller scale because nowhere else had a large group of identical teenagers like ours. It was reflected in the road accidents. In 1996 casualties were fifty percent higher than in the previous year and people argued whether it was due to

THC. In 1997 they'd increased again, almost reaching the 1973 level, and the compulsory chromatography test was introduced with random spot checks, but it didn't do much good. Then half-way through 1998 the Jonson-Ballard Act was hastily repealed and the recommendations of the Neville Committee were implemented. This meant that all drugs and intoxicants were legalized but with very heavy excise duty proportional to their estimated degree of harmfulness and it soon produced the stable situation which prevails today. We had other problems as well though.

One evening in the Christmas holiday I went to the Women's Institute to hear a lecture on 'Eclipsing Binaries and other Multiple Stars'. There was quite a surge of public interest in astronomy around that time you remember, with the most unlikely groups of people listening to erudite lectures on the subject. But our speaker didn't turn up; he was flying himself up from Manchester and we found out afterwards that he had run out of fuel and landed his copter in a field eighteen miles away. Anyway we waited for over an hour and then had our biscuits and coffee and all went home.

I'd left Richard doing his homework but when I got back to the cottage there were no lights on so I let myself in and called out to see if he were anywhere about. There was no reply and I went up to find out if he'd gone to bed. I didn't knock in case he was asleep but quietly opened the door and put my head round. In the light from the landing I could see two figures on the bed and a touch of the switch revealed that they were Richard and Sally, both as naked as new-born babies.

'I think you had better get dressed and then come down and tell me all about it,' I said grimly, and marched back down to the sitting-room, where I was joined a few minutes later by the only slightly penitent young couple.

'I'm sorry Mrs Bradwell. We didn't mean to shock you,' said Sally. 'I was going home before you came back but you're earlier than we expected.'

'The lecturer didn't turn up,' I informed them, 'but

that's not really the point. We're not living in 1980 you know. We reckon to have certain standards of behaviour now.'

'Sally and I love one another,' Richard announced.

'Oh yes. Big deal. I've heard that before. It's like something out of the Sunday papers. Didn't you learn in school about the social destructiveness of sexual promiscuity?'

'We're not promiscuous. We love one another. We're going to be married one day and we shall always be faithful to one another.'

'You're not in a position to get married yet and you might change your mind before then.'

'We shan't, we shan't, we shan't,' they repeated together in unison, clinging to one another for moral support.

'Suppose Sally becomes pregnant. What will the position be then?'

'She couldn't Helen. I've had a reversible vasoblock.'

'You've what?'

'I've been temporarily sterilized. We all have, at birth. Mr Tranter told us in the human biology classes. He said it's nothing to worry about because it's a very simple matter to undo it when the time comes for us to have our babies, but he said they thought it was the safest thing just to make sure nobody had an accident.'

'He did, did he? I'll have a word with Mr Tranter tomorrow.'

'But there's no harm in it, Helen, if Sally can't get pregnant, and we can't be spreading venereal disease because neither of us has had anything to do with anyone else. And we love one another, Helen, so what's the harm?'

'I'll tell you what's the harm,' I said as calmly as I could. 'Human happiness in this life depends on love between men and women, and the only reliable basis for that love is pair-bonding, a permanent commitment of a man and a woman to one another, whether you call it marriage or something else. Promiscuous sexual activity weakens that bond, it degrades the act of love and thereby diminishes human happiness.'

141

'But we're not promiscuous Mrs Bradwell. Richard and I will always be faithful to one another.'

'How can you say that when you're not yet seventeen, you stupid little baggage?' I shouted with a vehemence I regretted at once.

Richard sprang to her aid and his bitterness surprised me. 'Well if you're so hot on life-long love what happened to George Bradwell? Why did you send him away? And why didn't you marry him properly in the first place? Is five years what you call faithful for ever? When Sally and I get married it will be for always.'

'I wanted to marry George properly,' I explained, crushed by Richard's attack. 'I would have but there were terrible difficulties and complications, things you don't understand about.'

'I'm sorry about everything Mrs Bradwell,' Sally said. 'I think I had better go now.'

'Richard will see you home, but just mind what you're up to on the way, and I'll expect him back in half an hour.'

When they had gone I sat on the settee, trembling with emotion, and tried to analyse my reactions. I had been quite right to let them see that I disapproved of their behaviour but I felt shocked at the depth of my own feelings, and I realized with shame that I was jealous. I envied them their happiness. I almost hated Sally for loving Richard, and when I remembered that Richard was really Andrew I felt my mind and my heart tied up in knots of confusion. But at least I was beginning to understand myself now.

When I could think a little more coolly I realized that there were still many things about all the boys and girls that I didn't understand. It wasn't just Richard and Sally. The way the boys and girls had paired off so firmly at such an early age, the way they felt they belonged to one another, the way each boy could pick out his girl-friend instantly although others might think them almost identical, all these were questions that should have an answer. The person who would give it to me was Dr Franks. He had been so forthcoming in his explanation about the cloning and incubation I felt sure he would be willing to explain a bit more, and he was.

'Why of course Mrs Bradwell, it's the specific pheromones.'

'Oh yes. How silly of me not to realize when the explanation is so simple,' I laughed. 'What are pheromones?'

'A pheromone is a chemical substance produced by one animal which has a certain effect on another animal. It's an ectohormone.'

'Yes,' I said.

'It can be any effect but it's usually attraction or repulsion, most commonly sexual attraction.'

'Like "Parisian Nights"?' I suggested.

'I have never experienced that particular olfactory passion-rouser myself,' he admitted, 'but I imagine it's something like that. Do you know a male rhinoceros can detect the presence of a female rhinoceros at a distance of goodness knows how many yards in the deepest jungle.'

'But what's that got to do with the boys and girls?'

'Ah well, because of civilization and so on natural pheromones probably play a relatively minor role in human encounters. That's why they need a bit of help from "Parisian Nights".'

'Most boys and girls manage to get together quick enough but this lot seem as if they've had an overdose of something.'

'It may be,' he pondered, 'but I don't think they'll be any the worse for it.'

'I still don't understand how they come to have this special individual attraction for one another.'

'Another piece of genetic engineering I'm afraid, but this really was essential. You see with thirty women almost identical and thirty men equally similar the confusion on that space-ship would have been unimaginable. So by a piece of incredibly delicate micro-manipulation the genes determining their sexual pheromones were subtly altered so that each girl is attractive to only one of the boys, and vice versa.'

'That's certainly the way it's worked out,' I agreed.

'Anyway you know as much about it as I do now, Mrs Bradwell, and as you see we'll have to be a little bit tolerant about them jumping into bed with one another. By the way. Did they tell you? There's no danger of any untoward happy events because the boys have all had a little operation. It's completely reversible, of course.'

Well I was somewhat enlightened. I was still terribly jealous of Sally but at least now I recognized it and understood it. And she really was a very sweet girl. I couldn't have picked a nicer and more suitable wife for Richard.

Chapter fifteen

I HAD always hoped that Richard would go to college but I realized I wasn't going to have much say in it, and in any case I assumed it would be a question of them either all going or none. The trouble was that I couldn't see the Space Station authorities letting them out of their sight while they spent three or four years at Oxford or Cambridge, even Glasgow or Edinburgh.

It had been a great surprise to see the subjects the clone children chose to specialize in when they went into the sixth form at school. Naturally I had assumed that they would lean heavily towards physics, astronomy, mathematics, in fact anything related to space-flight, but exactly the reverse was true; the most popular subjects were history, and English and American literature. I had also supposed that, being so similar, they would all want to take the same subjects, but again I was mistaken. Even the ones taking history studied different periods and those doing English literature chose different set books. Richard explained.

'It's no good my doing the Middle Ages, Helen. Stanley's doing that and it would be a waste of time for me to learn what he already knows.'

'Would it?' I enquired.

'Of course. If there's anything about the Middle Ages I want to know I've only got to ask Stanley.'

In the sixth form Richard took Early English history, music, and symbolic logic. Sally studied the geography of South America, Latin, and plant physiology. There weren't any two children who took the same combination of subjects.

At the time when Richard was starting in the lower sixth form the eldest boys and girls had just left to go to college. Of course you can guess where they all went – the

University of Bannockside. It's world famous now and I expect you'd be surprised to learn that six months before it opened there wasn't one stone standing on another. Even when work started on it everybody assumed that it was just another extension to the Space Station. As a matter of fact now that the work at the Station is finishing the rumour is that the University is going to take over the whole lot, to make the biggest teaching complex outside Brazil. But that's for the future; I was telling you about nineteen ninety seven.

Bannockside University was built specially for the clone children but it was designed to take a lot more than sixty students. None of the other local children were allowed to go there though; those who were considered to merit a university education went off to Edinburgh or Aberdeen, some to London or Manchester. The places were filled by students from all over the Federation, from everywhere except Russia, China, and the African Communist Republic.

'You see Helen,' Richard explained, 'we must get to know people from every culture over the whole world. Dr Franks says he would like us to meet Russians and Chinese but if he let them come to Bannockside they might send our secrets back to their own space scientists.'

I was aware of a disquieting intensity of purpose about all the children now. 'It's very nice to meet people from other countries,' I said, 'and I'm sure you'll find it very interesting.'

'But it's more than just that, Mrs Bradwell,' Sally told me. 'We shall be custodians of the culture of the whole world.'

I suppose it's natural for young people of that age to have an inflated idea of their own importance, but I did wonder whether it was just that, and my spine chilled with a tiny shiver of apprehension at the intensity of their expressions.

*　　*　　*

I still heard from George from time to time, twice a year

146

to be precise, on the occasion of Christmas and my birthday; he always sent me a small present with just a card expressing his best wishes. I had thought he would have married again. I had hoped he could have found a wife who could love him as he deserved, but I gathered that he was still on his own.

On my birthday that year George wrote me a short letter with the gloves he sent as a present.

'Dear Helen, I hope you and Richard are both well. He must be quite a young man now. Forgive my bothering you with a letter but I feel I must tell everyone my good news. I have managed to get back into private practice, and in the Lake District of all places. I am going into a partnership in Ambleside and I can't tell you how happy I am to be leaving the insane frenzy of London for civilized Cumbria. If you should ever pass this way call in and see the surgery; it's what you might call traditional modern style.'

Poor George. I still had a conscience about the way I'd treated him, even without Richard's reminding me.

*　　*　　*

At the University as at school every one of the children took a different course, but they all obtained the same degree, Bachelor of Knowledge. Although they were equally intelligent they didn't get the same grades because some had taken courses less suited to their abilities. Most of the boys who took mathematical or scientific subjects got firsts or upper seconds whereas those taking history or English ended up with lower seconds or thirds, but they all accepted it philosophically.

'I know Helen,' Richard explained. 'I should quite likely have got a grade one in physics but it doesn't matter. There are four or five physicists of one kind or another but I'm the only one in the whole group studying that particular period in history so my contribution to society is infinitely greater than if I were just duplicating somebody else's knowledge.'

I must admit I found such seriousness out of place in one so young, and I found the assumption that the world consisted of only sixty people faintly alarming. It almost seemed as if the rest of humanity were going to be wiped out and Richard and his friends were being groomed to take over the world. And yet when I looked at Richard and Sally, saw their happy smiles, heard their warm friendly voices, observed their affection for one another, for their friends and for me, I could not believe that any sinister purpose lay behind them.

They all enjoyed their three years at college immensely, and so they should have because the University of Bannockside, with its teaching staff from all over the globe, was a wonderful place. I remember during Richard's first year, that was the University's third year, going to the open day.

'There won't be much to see in the History Department,' Richard warned me. I wasn't expecting much there but, in fact, the collection of models, pictures, manuscripts, archeological finds, old coins and so on, was excellent, displayed with brilliance and calculated to persuade the most reluctant historian that here was a subject of great intellectual fascination whose study held the key to everything we know in life today.

However, one could admit, I suppose, that the History Section was dull by comparison with most of the other subjects. The 3D back-projection slides with sound and smell, commonplace today, were novel enough then to make the Geography display noteworthy, the ingenious changing patterns demonstrating the new chameleon-dyestuffs in the Chemistry Department, and the working model of a fusion generator in the Physics Department were worth more than a second glance, but what attracted most of the public interest was the Astronomy Section.

It was entitled "The Planets of Other Stars" and consisted of a series of 3D colour pictures, without sound and smell of course, of about fifteen other solar systems. They were not as needle-sharp as the ones in the Geography Department, but vastly brighter and clearer than I should evcr have imagined possible. One of the lecturers explained how they were made but it was a bit over my head although perhaps it makes sense to you.

'They're just computer-integrated multiple-exposure pictures,' he said, 'like spectroscopists use to record infrared spectra of nanogram samples.' Don't worry if that doesn't mean anything to you because it didn't to me, although I did get a bit of the drift of the idea when Sally explained it to me afterwards.

'What they do, you see Mrs Bradwell, is to take a lot of pictures of the same star with the most powerful telescopes in all the orbital laboratories including the two moon bases. They don't bother with photos from Earth because atmosphere would spoil those.'

'Yes,' I agreed, doubtfully.

'Now you can magnify an image or enlarge a picture as many times as you like to make it as big as you want but the trouble is that it gets more and more blurred so you still can't see any more detail.'

'No,' I agreed.

'That's due to random noise, optical imperfections, grain, aberration and so on, but if you take a thousand pictures, say a hundred from each of ten observatories, scan them with a high-resolution videocam, and convert each to a digital code, you can feed these codings into a computer, can't you?'

'Can you?'

'Of course. Why not? The computer can pick out the essential features common to all the pictures, rejecting the noise and fuzziness which varies from one picture to another, and then an ordinary video decoder changes the result back to a picture again.'

'How far away are those other worlds?' I asked them.

'Ten light years, twenty light years I suppose,' said Richard casually.

'What's that in English?'

'A couple of hundred million million kilometres.'

'And are there people living on these planets?'

They both laughed.

149

'They haven't got the magnification up to that yet,' Richard informed me, 'but anyway most of them are either too hot or too cold, or the atmosphere's poisonous or there isn't an atmosphere at all, or there's too much radiation or no water. Only a very small proportion of them would be suitable for supporting life, and I suppose some small fraction of those would actually have life on.'

'Even then it probably wouldn't be the sort of life you would classify as people,' Sally added.

I thought that for an historian and a plant physiologist they were remarkably well informed about astronomy, but then they would be wouldn't they?

'What about our Sun's other planets?' I asked. 'What about Jupiter? Could life survive there?'

'Not a chance,' said Richard. 'There's not a proper solid surface to it for a start.'

'There's always the moons,' Sally suggested.

'That's true, but we aren't supposed to talk about them, are we?' He turned to me. 'It's completely pointless, I know, but for some silly reason Dr Franks has asked us not to talk about the moons of Jupiter.'

'Well I think it's a red. . . .'

'Hush!' Richard silenced her.

*　　*　　*

At the end of Richard's first year at college the eldest of the children were just leaving with the first degrees awarded by the University of Bannockside. The day after graduation they had another ceremony, a multiple wedding at the local church. Ten boys married ten girls, the ones they had been going steady with for the last ten years. Personally I thought it was about time they made it official.

Weddings, which had become very informal in the nineteen eighties, especially with the introduction of limited-term contracts, were now becoming a lot more formal again, almost like the old black and white weddings. It was fashionable for the bridegroom to wear a suit of dark green, red, or blue, perhaps deep purple, rich orange-brown, or yellow-grey. Then the bride would wear an old-fashioned looking dress in a very pale pastel shade of the same colour. Church ceremonies had become more usual again too, you remember.

Everyone in Bannockside wanted to see the wedding; it was the most spectacular event the place had ever known. Only the adopted families of the brides and bridegrooms and their close relatives were to be accommodated in the church itself, although at the last moment it was decided that the other forty members of the clones could be squeezed in. There wasn't room for their families of course.

I should have liked to be in the church, and I thought about claiming that I was a special case, but I decided not to. After all I should be able to go in two years time when Richard and Sally were married.

A lot of people were watching from home because the local video station was covering the event very fully, but I decided I wanted to be actually there, and I managed to get a very good spot on the other side of the road right opposite the church door.

I got there almost two hours before the ceremony was to begin but my long wait was amply rewarded when the ten brides arrived each wearing a different pastel shade, each in the traditional glass-covered electric float with her father. They were beautiful, but then all brides are beautiful; even I had been beautiful on my wedding day.

After they'd all gone in I settled down to another long wait. It was to be a full-length perpetual-contract ceremony as was usual again by then. In any case the children of the clones would never have pledged themselves for anything less than eternity. With ten contracts to be sealed I knew it would be over an hour but at last the church doors were opened again and I heard the tone-synthesiser playing Mendelssohn's Wedding March.

The ten couples came out arm in arm and formed a long line in front of the porch. The men wore very formal suits, each a different colour, the brides beautiful pastel gowns with old-fashioned head-dresses, and each carried a

151

bouquet of different coloured flowers. I looked along the line at the ten handsome grooms and the ten beautiful brides and I suddenly knew I was looking at something that had happened before. It was a long time ago, but I'd still got the photograph to prove it.

Chapter sixteen

EVEN NOW I can hardly believe that it could have taken me so long to recognize whose cells the girls had come from. It must have been obvious to everyone else for years, and it was no wonder the old director had tried to avoid embarrassment by pushing me off to London. The only excuse for myself I can think of is that I must have had some kind of psychological block; I was blind to what I didn't want to see. After all I'd realized years before that the boys were Andrew.

'You've known for a long time, haven't you?' I asked Sally. She and Richard had found me wandering absently outside the church and were now reviving me with cups of warm sweet tea at home.

'Yes Helen, I've known for a very long time and I've wanted to tell you but they said we must wait. What made you suddenly guess today?'

'Today even I couldn't miss it. Let me show you something.'

My old photographs were in the bottom of a chest of drawers in the bedroom and it didn't take me long to find the wedding group.

'It's wonderful to know that I shall be as beautiful as that on my wedding day,' Sally said. 'Please don't cry Helen. It isn't anything sad, is it? It makes me very happy to know that I'm someone as kind and beautiful as you.'

*   *   *

Besides being a great shock it was very very puzzling and I decided I should have to try and find out how it had come about, or rather why it had. I went to see Dr Franks again.

'You mustn't be upset about it, Mrs Bradwell,' he told me. 'It's really a very great honour. By the way, I'm sorry I had to prevaricate slightly when you asked me who the girls were, but I'd had strict instructions. I don't think I actually told you any lies.'

'I don't think you did,' I admitted.

'I do realize the emotional stress it involves, particularly with the boys being your dead husband but of course I had nothing to do with the original decision. That was all before my time and no one knew then that Ebenezer was going to lose his life in such a tragic way.'

'Do you know anything about the decisions taken at the very beginning?' I asked him.

'Well I received a thorough briefing from Dr Sanders when I took over, and I've got minutes of all the meetings and reports of decisions in my files. What was it you wanted to know?'

'Just how they came to pick Andrew, Eb that is, and me. You remember saying they chose the genotype, is that what you call it, they chose each of the genotypes secretly from about three hundred thousand organ-donor volunteers.'

'Yes that's right.'

'So the odds against getting a particular husband and wife would be ninety thousand million to one, and even after you'd chosen the man, if you take that as read, the odds against getting his wife with the second selection are still three hundred thousand to one.'

'Mrs Bradwell, your probability theory is impeccable.'

'Well what about it? I'm quite prepared to believe in minor miracles and small coincidences but there is a limit.'

'That's exactly what I said to Dr Sanders when I heard about it.'

'And what did he say?'

'He said that it was a long story.'

'I'll bet it was, but did he tell it to you?'

'He did, and I rather get the impression that I'm going to have to tell it to you,' he laughed.

'I know you're a very busy man, but I should be very grateful if you could.'

He looked at his watch. 'I have a committee meeting in

twenty-five minutes but I can spare the time until then.'
He rang a bell on his desk and a secretary appeared at once.

'Miss Betts. Would you run a file-tape search between nineteen seventy-five and nineteen eighty, and bring me a printout of anything with the coding for Genotype Selection.'

'Yes Dr Franks.'

'And while we're waiting for that will you please ask Mrs Duke to bring in the coffee.'

The coffee appeared almost at once on a beautiful silver tray. I think that was the last time I ever saw silver used for purely decorative purposes, and it had actually been classified as E.P.O., essential purposes only, several years before that. As well as the coffee the tray also bore a large dish of chocolate biscuits, marshmallows, and meringues. He does himself proud, I thought, but in fact Dr Franks didn't touch anything except a cup of black coffee.

Before I'd finished the second biscuit Miss Betts returned with a folded length of computer paper and the Director looked quickly through it.

'I didn't really need this, because I can remember it all, but I might as well get the details right. As I think you know, the problem was to select men and women for the crew of a space-ship.'

'Yes.'

'It wasn't too difficult to write down specifications for the ideal space-man. Strength, agility, resistance to temperature variation, resistance to stress, courage, intelligence, ingenuity, determination, you name it and we'd like it. The only problem might have been the relative importance of competing virtues but anyway they sorted that out and, after physical and mental tests on all the unsuspecting volunteers, as well as chromosomic analysis, the computer selected Genotype 129317, which was your Eb. It's rather heart-warming that after all the high-powered selection they should come up with what seemed like a perfect ordinary guy. You might have thought it would be some kind of Mr Universe.'

155

'Andrew was no ordinary guy, Dr Franks. But what about the girls?'

'Nobody had any idea what an ideal space-woman would be like, or at any rate they'd all got different ideas. Some said she had to be big and strong, others thought she should be small. Some favoured mental toughness, others opted for warmth and kindness. Apparently the committee was at it for five days and they still hadn't decided whether they wanted a champion athlete, a sort of Florence Nightingale, a sex kitten, a female genius, or a good cook.'

'Which am I?'

'None of them, or all of them. What happened was that somebody suggested that the most important thing of all was that the man and woman should suit one another, and this was agreed.'

'Yes.'

'Genotype 129317 had already been selected so the computer was simply programmed to screen the female candidates for the most suitable mate, if you'll forgive the expression.'

The Director glanced at his notes. 'Yes here it is. They used a programme based on the old Wilson-Grundig Compatability Formula and the computer selected Genotype 485632.'

'Me?'

'When they told Dr Sanders he wouldn't believe it. He thought they were pulling his leg. It was like a modern day fairy story, only Dr Sanders doesn't believe in fairies so he made a few enquiries.'

'And what did he find?'

'That you and Dr Garth had been introduced by an organization called "Digital Dating Inc.", using the Wilson-Grundig Programme on an I.C.M. 746 Computer.'

'It's a small world, isn't it?'

'More a question of great minds thinking alike, even electronic minds.'

*   *   *

156

The boys and girls, young men and young women now, who had graduated that year had gone straight on to the staff of the Space Station for their final specialized training.

It seemed terrible the way their future was all mapped out without their even being consulted, and the way everyone had to conform to exactly the same system. You would have thought that a group of sixty people would have had different interests; some would have wanted to be astronauts perhaps but others would have wanted to be actors, or teachers, or doctors, farmers, musicians, or business men. Instead they were all forced to work at the Space Station and I couldn't even understand who was forcing them. Richard didn't look at it like that though.

'It's not a question of being forced, Helen. We want to.'

'All of you?'

'Of course. Since we're all the same person it's obvious we should want to do the same thing, and since Ebenezer Garth wanted to work at the Space Station it's obvious that we should want to. The boys want to anyway and the girls want to be with the boys.'

'You've all taken different subjects at college.'

'That's so there should be no duplication. We shall be custodians of the world's culture and between us we have to cover as much of the world's knowledge and wisdom as we possibly can. So we all specialize in different subjects.'

'What about the rest of us? Isn't the world's culture and wisdom safe with us?'

'You'll be back on Earth.'

'And you'll be travelling to Jupiter, but you won't need a knowledge of Byzantine art for that, and we shall still be here when you get back, at least I sincerely hope so.'

Richard was silent for a while. He looked very serious.

'Helen. Dear Helen. There's more to it than you know about.'

'What else is there?'

'I think it would be best if Peter told you about it.'

'Peter?'

'Peter McLellan. He's going to show Sally and me some

new 3D slides up at the Station this evening and I know he wouldn't mind if you came.'

'Peter McLellan. Of course I remember him. He's working at the Space Station already.'

'Yes. Isn't he lucky, and I've got over a year before I can start.'

It was almost the only time I heard an expression of envy from one of the children about any of the others, but apparently the younger ones still at college were very keen to join their elder brothers at the Station. It had been arranged that each of the twenty already there should entertain two of the younger ones for an informal exposition of their work.

'You'd better ask Peter if he minds if I come too,' I suggested.

'There's no need. He won't mind.'

'But you'd better make sure.'

'I am sure. I know how Peter's brain works because it works the same as mine so I know he'll be delighted to see you.'

He was too.

'Good evening Mrs Bradwell. I'm so glad you could come as well. I was hoping you would.'

We had met just outside the main gate and, seeing us with Peter, the guards waved us all through.

'I've booked one of the small projection rooms,' Peter informed us, 'and we've got about fifteen new slides that you haven't seen yet. They've just come through, and they're out of this world.'

'I hoped they would be,' Sally murmured, and they all laughed.

The viewing-room was fitted with twelve luxurious armchairs facing a translucent wall, on the other side of which was the back-projector. The end seat on the front row, where Peter sat, had a tiny control panel on one arm and with this Peter could change slides, focus, alter the magnification and colour balance, and so on. The equipment is much more common now but when it first came out it was considered very advanced.

158

'They're full five-sense pictures,' Peter told us, 'but most of it's pure imagination, poetic licence or what have you. The actual pictures are completely authentic but the sound, smell, taste, and touch are all just artist's impression, based on spectroscopic data mainly.'

Peter touched the keys on his switch-board, the room lights dimmed, and a spot of light appeared on the screen. As we watched the spot grew larger and resolved itself into seven smaller ones which in turn grew larger until all but one had moved right off the screen. Then that continued to grow until I saw that it was like a picture of the Earth taken from space. There were continents and oceans but I couldn't make out which they were. I felt a warm breeze on my cheek, and a slightly salt taste in my mouth. I heard the sound of birds and of running water, and I smelled a mixture of heather and orange blossom.

'They certainly went to town with the effects,' Richard commented.

'They're pure artist's imagination,' Peter apologized. 'It might not be anything like that at all. Shall I switch them off?'

'Oh no,' Sally and I protested.

'It's beautiful,' Sally added.

I still couldn't make out the continents. 'Is it Earth?' I asked.

'No, Mrs Bradwell. It's Eden,' Peter explained.

'Eden? You mean the Garden of Eden?'

'Of course not, Helen. It's the planet Eden.'

For no apparent reason a shiver chilled my spine. A nameless fear raced my heart. 'Where is it?' I asked.

'I think it would be best if I showed you all the slides and then Richard and I will tell you about Eden,' said Peter.

The other slides were similar to the first but showed different sides of the planet as it rotated on its axis and orbited its star. They were all equally beautiful but the slide technicians had used different effects of sound, smell, taste and touch for each.

'Now tell me about it,' I said, my heart sick with irrational apprehension of what I should hear.

'We're going there, Helen. We're all going to Eden.'

The news was no shock, just a crystallization of an intuitive fear that had been with me for a very long time.

'You mean you're going to Eden in the space rocket?'

'I'm sorry Mrs Bradwell. Please don't be upset. It's our destiny.'

'But I thought the rocket was going to Jupiter.'

'It's called the Jupiter Mission but that's just its name. It doesn't mean we're going there,' Peter explained.

'They probably hope that people will think that though,' Sally added. 'It's really a blind, a red herring, isn't it?'

Although I had feared something of the sort the full implications were only just penetrating my mind. 'If you go to another star, to another planetary system, you won't be back for years and years,' I wept.

'Helen. Dear Helen,' said Richard gently. 'We shan't be coming back at all. It's fifteen light-years and we shall only be going at half the speed of light. That's thirty years in your frame of reference and twenty-six in ours, even allowing for the Lorentz transformation, so we shall be old by the time we get there. It's a one-way trip, Helen.'

His words echoed back over twenty years, and I remembered the phrase Andrew had used after his space-medicine tests.

'It's a colonization project,' Peter explained. 'We're going to start a colony on that planet you saw on the slides. Isn't that the most exciting thing in the world?' he added, unaware of the irony in his words.

'But fifteen light-years. Why did they have to choose somewhere so far away?'

'It's the nearest planet that's enough like Earth to support a colony. At least as far as we know it will.'

'And if it won't?'

'If there's some undetected toxic factor in the atmosphere, or in the unlikely event of its being inhabited and the natives' being hostile we just put the ship into orbit and live out the rest of our lives like that. There's no other likely planet near.'

'How did they know you would want to go to Eden?'

Richard looked at me almost defiantly. 'We said we would go. We volunteered to go.'

'We all volunteered,' said Sally, her words stabbing my heart with a dagger of remorse. 'We all volunteered before we were born, didn't we?'

*   *   *

Gradually I got used to the idea that in a few years time I should have to say goodbye to Richard for ever. The sadness hung over me, but sometimes I could forget it for several hours on end. In any case I was determined to enjoy the years that remained and I begrudged every wasted second that brought the parting nearer.

But time passed rapidly and Richard and Sally left the University to join the staff of the Space Station. Once again the day after the graduation ceremony saw another multiple wedding at St. Giles' Church. The bridegrooms were just as handsome as in the two previous years, the brides were every bit as beautiful, and this time I was a guest of honour. I had a seat in the church and, of course, I went to the reception.

It was at the reception that I disgraced myself, and I don't know whether you'd think it excused it or made it worse to say that I was drunk at the time. Alcohol was back again after the short spell of world-wide prohibition but I had never been used to drinking much. Four glasses of malt champagne were more than enough to annihilate my sense of propriety, so expecting me to make a short speech was asking for trouble. I can't remember all that I said but I know there was a lot of muttering and drawing-in of breath going on. There was a bit about Adam and Eve and I think I was saying something about Jupiter having red spots and red herrings when suddenly the toastmaster got up and hit the table with his gavel.

'Pray silence for the next speaker.'

'Here! I haven't finished yet,' I shouted, but I had

161

finished. Slowly I subsided into my chair and slid off it under the table.

Nobody said anything about it afterwards, which was very kind of them all, but when Richard and Sally came back from their honeymoon in the Mid-Atlantic Hilton I felt I ought to apologize.

'Don't worry, Helen,' Richard said. 'Nobody minded, and I thought you were very good. That toastmaster was an old stuffed shirt trying to shut you up.'

'It wasn't quite all true though, was it?' Sally said.

'What wasn't?'

'That stuff about the distant patter of tiny feet, and repopulating the gardens of Eden.'

'Did I say that? No wonder they wanted to stop me. But why is it not true?'

'Eden is to be populated from the sperm and egg banks.'

'The what?'

'The sperm and egg banks. Did you think we were going to fill up the entire planet with our own children?'

'Not all at once, but gradually over a number of generations.'

'There wouldn't be enough genetic variety,' Richard said. 'Our children wouldn't be as much alike as we are, but their characteristics would come from a very small pool of genes.'

'How would that matter?'

Sally enlightened me. 'Apart from it being a bit boring, not to say confusing, having a whole planet full of people who all look alike, you need the variety to provide means of adaptation. The chances are we shan't be quite the type of people best suited for life on Eden, but with enough genetic variety natural selection can sort out the strains able to do best.'

Richard went on. 'After we've built some kind of shelter, established the necessary life-support facilities, sowed our wheat, potatoes and so on, and grown up the deep-freeze embryos of the domestic and farm animals, breeding out from the sperm and egg banks will be our first job. We're taking all the incubators we need, and

162

within a year or two of landing we shall all have our little families of adopted boys and girls.'

Sally and Richard appeared to be delighted at the prospect, but I can't say that I was overjoyed.

'Do you mean you aren't going to have any children the ordinary old-fashioned way?'

'Oh yes. We're planning two for each couple,' Sally informed me, 'some time during the first five years of the voyage.'

I didn't say anything, but I suppose I must have looked slightly incredulous.

'Well the journey will take thirty years, Helen, and we shall be over fifty when we get there, so we'll be glad of some younger hands to help with the work.'

'Of course,' I agreed. 'Anyway, don't forget to send me an invitation to the christening.'

Chapter seventeen

RICHARD AND Sally were married in 2001, four years before they were to leave the Earth on their one-way trip. All the members of the clones were now on the staff of the Space Station, and a special block of flats had been built for them. I still saw quite a lot of Richard and Sally; they used to come to the cottage for lunch every Saturday and I had supper with them in the flat on Wednesdays. I missed Richard but they were both so wonderfully happy I couldn't regret Richard's leaving home, and now that I knew Sally was me I didn't feel any jealousy; it seemed rather that I was sharing in her happiness.

I was still teaching at the Dunburn Senior School. Now that Richard and all his friends had left I thought about asking if I could go back to Bannockside Primary. It would have been a lot nearer but I had found teaching the older children more interesting.

Travelling was expensive; power was twelve pence a megajoule but I'd changed the car again, for a battery-pedal runabout of the type that is so popular today. The sulphur-sodium cells were a big improvement on the old lead-acid ones, and, for maintaining a modest speed on the flat, pedalling was not too hard. The big advantage was that although you used power to accelerate or for going up a hill when you decelerated or came down the hill it would automatically switch to generate and put the power back into the battery.

All the young couples had different sports and hobbies. I think, once again, they were trying to make sure that between them they covered as many as possible of the world's leisure-time activities. Some enjoyed sailing, others cycling, a few went in for athletics, and others occupied themselves with gliding or ice-skating. I couldn't see how they were going to do any of these on Eden, certainly not on the ship that took them there, but perhaps they were just trying to make the most of their last few years on Earth.

Richard and Sally were mad keen on hot-air ballooning. This had had a steady vogue since its revival around 1970, but the thermal grid gave it a tremendous boost. Instead of relying on a wicked-looking gas burner to heat the air all you had to do was fill up with hot air from a grid terminal. Using the new zero-conductivity fabrics for the envelope made it possible to retain the heat almost indefinitely and extended the range enormously. Nobody had found a way of sailing a balloon against the wind though; Richard used to say they were working on it, but I didn't give much for their chances.

Except in the rare case of a complete change-round of the wind you can never fly a balloon back to the place it started from, so if Richard and Sally wanted to fly together they had to get someone to tow the trailer out to where they landed and bring everything back. They could usually find one of their friends to do this but if not I used to help out. In the summer when the weather was nice it was quite pleasant to follow the balloon with the car and trailer but otherwise I stayed at home and waited for Richard to ring up with his portable radio-phone link and let me know where they'd landed.

The spring and summer of 2005 were dull and wet but we had a week of glorious sunshine at the beginning of May.

'Can you come out and pick us up tomorrow, Helen?' Richard asked me that Saturday.

'Yes of course. I'll come and watch. It's such lovely weather perhaps it'll cheer me up.'

I certainly needed cheering up; I'd never really got over the breakdown I'd had the previous year. It seemed so silly to be the way I was. I'd only got Richard for a few more months, perhaps weeks because the date of the launch still hadn't been announced, and I knew I ought to be bright and cheerful so that at least I could enjoy the days that remained. Dr Slade, who'd taken over Dr Lowrey's prac-

165

tice, had said I'd be all right if only I'd take my happiness pills, but I didn't want to. I'd seen too many people who couldn't do without them. In any case if I took the pills I couldn't drive the car.

'I'm surprised the medical profession haven't developed some without the side-effects,' I said.

'They aren't side-effects, Mrs Bradwell. The old pills used to cause things like drowsiness, but this is a different problem altogether.'

'What do you mean?'

'Well they're intended to make you so you don't mind what happens. If you don't mind what happens you don't mind having an accident, and if you don't mind having an accident you're not safe to drive a car.'

'I see. Anyway I'm afraid that if I start taking them regularly I shall get to depend on them.'

Dr Slade looked at me thoughtfully. 'There is the Memory Deletion Centre, you know. They've achieved remarkable results in several cases I've heard of.'

But I mustn't think about Dr Slade. It was the first weekend in May and the weather was perfect.

Richard and Sally always took off from the field by the side of the loch. There was a coin-slot thermal tap on the main road within reach of their hose so they could get all the hot air they needed to keep them up for at least two hours. Although they usually took off from the same place they always came down somewhere different, depending mainly on the direction of the wind.

I helped them fill the vast blue and gold envelope, anchored to one of the stanchions – it was an official take-off site – and then stowed the hose in the trailer, while Richard and Sally made themselves comfortable in the basket. A narrow pennant on top of the balloon showed which way they would be going; it would hang limply as soon as they were drifting free.

'We're about ready then,' Richard called out.

'See you in time for tea,' shouted Sally.

'Cheerio,' I answered. 'Take care. Watch the pylons and don't fall out.'

Richard released the rope and, with gathering speed, the ornamented silken bag lifted its human cargo above the trees, above the houses and up into the hills.

One day soon they would make a very different ascent, not lifted gently by a beautiful sphere of warm air, but hurtled violently on a pillar of blast and fire, not for an hour of pleasure to be back in time for tea, but on a one-way trip to an unknown world. I wished it could all have been just ballooning.

The blue and gold balloon rose at an angle of about ten degrees to the vertical and levelled out at about a thousand feet. Richard could control the buoyancy with a small compressor, pumping some of the air into an in-sulated cylinder when they reached a suitable height, releasing it back to the envelope when more lift was required. They were heading directly over the Station site, now dominated by the towering mass of the Jupiter I rocket behind it. That was all a restricted area so it meant a considerable detour for me.

I wasn't using my own car; it hadn't a towing bracket and wouldn't have pulled the balloon trailer if it had. Richard had borrowed a van from the Station leisure club and this was much more suitable. Quickly I got in and headed for the Cranshaw Crossroads. If I turned right there I should be going parallel with the path of the balloon.

At the crossroads I stopped and looked out. The balloon was roughly where I had calculated but lower than I expected and losing height very rapidly, obviously in trouble. Every impulse bade me race off after it but I knew that I should lose them unless I waited. With agonized concern I watched as the gold and blue envelope, barely half inflated now, sank to the ground. It was about two kilometres ahead and a half to the right, I estimated. Desperately I pressed the starter relay and tore up the road until the clock showed another two point nought. There was a narrow track on the right, but would it take me to the right place? As I hesitated the ambulance roared overhead.

Now I was more worried than ever. They must be hurt. They must have telephoned for help on the radio-link.

The track was a bit rough, but passable, and a minute later I could see them. Between the upturned basket and the bright orange rescue craft I saw one figure on the ground and two bending over.

'It's all right, Helen,' Richard called to me. 'We're more or less in one piece only Sally's hurt her leg.'

I rushed to Sally and saw from the way she bit her lip that she was in great pain, but as I put my hand on her brow the ambulance-man was giving her a pain-killing injection.

'Just another few moments, my darling,' said Richard, and quite quickly Sally's face began to clear.

'Yes that's better,' she breathed with relief. 'I think I've broken it though.'

'What happened?' I asked them.

'We must have had a puncture. The air was pouring out like water from a colander and we came down a lot too quick for comfort.'

The ambulance-man took Sally to hospital and Richard went with them. I stayed to pack the balloon and basket into the trailer and trundle it all back along the track to the road.

*   *   *

Sally's leg was broken, as she feared, but it was a simple fracture that wouldn't keep her in hospital more than a few days, although the leg would be in plaster for some time after she came out.

Richard and I visited her every day that week and she was as bright and cheerful as anything. Richard came to lunch on Saturday and we went straight to the hospital afterwards.

'I think I shall be out on Tuesday,' Sally told us; 'but I shall have to borrow a stick to get about on.'

I was going to meet Richard at the hospital the next afternoon but at about half-past eleven in the morning he came to the cottage. The expression on his face was one that I hope I shall never see again on anyone.

'It's Sally,' I gasped. 'What's happened?'

'It isn't that,' he said grimly. 'We take off on Wednesday morning.'

So that was it. This was what I woke up in the night screaming about. Those were the words I had been dreading for the last four years. But I wrestled with the implications. 'Sally. What about Sally? She won't be fit.'

'Sally will have to stay.'

'Well what about you? Are you staying too?'

'I must go with my friends, Helen. It is my duty, and even if it were not I could not bear to be parted from them.'

It didn't seem like Richard. It didn't sound like Richard. I would have said that no mortal thing could have parted him from Sally and here he was cheerfully talking about flying off and leaving her behind. Perhaps not cheerfully, but talking about it.

'How can you possibly bring yourself to go and leave Sally?' I asked him. I knew Andrew would never have left me like that.

'They're giving me aversion therapy,' he explained simply.

'They're giving you what?'

'Aversion treatment to turn me against Sally so that I don't mind being parted from her. I've had two sessions so far and I'm having one more this afternoon and one tomorrow. It's the best solution, isn't it?'

*   *   *

Most of the important things that happened in the next few days will be familiar to you. I hope they are anyway because my recollections are not likely to be reliable. Most of the time I was stoned paralytic with Dr Slade's happiness pills, which I had been swallowing in handfuls.

The Jupiter Mission had been officially known to the public since 1975 but news about its progress was always rather vague and anybody who actually tried to pry into the details very quickly found himself up against a brick wall. In any case thirty years is a very long time for people to remain interested in something that has no actual bearing on their personal lives.

But the launch was on the Videonews that evening, in fact the launch was the news and from then on the place was over-run with reporters, cameramen, commentators, and ordinary sightseers, but hardly any of it registered with me. One of the few things I can remember was being at Dr Slade's.

'I'm glad to see you're taking the tablets, Mrs Bradwell,' he said, 'but they don't seem to be doing you any good, do they?'

'They're not bloody well likely to, are they?' I screamed at him. 'Happiness pills! Who told you you could get happiness out of a bottle?'

'That only leaves the memory deletion, I'm afraid.'

'Get lost,' I told him. 'Get bloody lost.'

'Now look Mrs Bradwell. I'm advising you in your own interest. Memory deletion is nothing to be afraid of. It's quite painless, and it's completely specific. It's not like in the old days when it made you forget everything, even your own name and how to speak your own language. They'll just gently erase all the painful memories of your first husband, and all that terrible business of your adopted son and his wife, but you'll still remember the simply happy things in your life.'

'Take a running jump at yourself,' I told him. 'Go and kick yourself in the teeth but get out of my hair. Drop dead, will you?'

'You know, Mrs Bradwell, it would be much the best if you undertook this treatment voluntarily but that isn't the only way, is it? I could get a warrant if necessary. I think I'll make you an appointment for Thursday afternoon. Would about half-past two be convenient?'

Chapter eighteen

I SAID goodbye to Richard on Monday evening. We didn't say much and it wasn't a very emotional goodbye. My mind was just numb, incapable of thought or emotion, paralysed by the shock of knowing the launch was so soon. I was desperately miserable at the prospect of losing Richard but the knowledge that he and Sally would soon be parted for ever distressed me infinitely more.

I'd run out of pills by now but I didn't bother about getting any more. They weren't doing any good, and anyway I wanted to be as sober and clear-minded as possible for Wednesday morning.

The crew of the rocket went aboard on Tuesday evening, and the whole of that night was occupied with the long count-down, with all the thousands of checks Richard had told me were required to make sure that nothing could possibly go wrong. Sally stayed with me at the cottage. I didn't know whether she would want to come and live with me. I thought it would be the best thing, but poor Sally was in no state to discuss the future.

Neither of us slept at all that night and at five o'clock I got up and took Sally a cup of tea.

'You want to stay in bed and watch it on the upstairs screen,' I suggested, 'so don't go getting up until I come back, because you're not very steady on your feet yet. I'll bring you a bit of breakfast before I go.'

It was still dark when I set off and as usual I had forgotten to check the batteries. They were half charged so I should just about make it, but I used the pedals as much as possible to be on the safe side. Richard had offered to get me a seat in the stands but I felt I couldn't bear to be with other people so he arranged for me to watch from a lonely spot in the Station grounds. It wasn't really near enough to see properly, but it had the advantage of being private.

I got to the top of Gorse Hill about half an hour before lift-off, and for a while I just sat in the car and shivered, wishing we still had the cosy heaters the old petrol cars had. I would have switched on the windscreen defroster to try and warm myself up but I daren't flatten the batteries any more. Through the window of the car was the distant silver-grey shape of the rocket, but I could see much more detail on my little portable video.

When the count-down clock in the corner of the screen had got to zero minus ten minutes I thought I had better get out and see what I could see. For my last birthday Richard had given me a beautiful new image-intensifier. They'd only been on the market for a year or two and there was no doubt about their superiority over the old optical devices. It was a strange present to give a middle-aged woman but I realized now that it would be my last link with him. It would give me contact with the ship that carried them away for perhaps another thirty sentimental seconds.

Even with the image-intensifier there wasn't much to see until the white vapour from the liquid oxygen indicated that the time was very close indeed. And then at last I saw the dense smoke and the fierce red flames of the first-stage motors, and the great tower of metal was slowly moving, incredibly slowly, then faster, then incredibly fast.

I watched through the electronic binoculars until the ship had become a thin fiery line, then a tiny dot, and then only the memory of a dot. That was it then. All I had now were memories and they upset me so much that I should have to give them up.

Then I thought about Sally. Poor Sally. She was my own flesh and blood. She was me. If I were upset at losing Richard how must she feel? I had been devastated when Andrew had died, and now Sally had lost Richard. He was not dead but something worse, rushing away at half the speed of light with not the least possibility of ever returning. I must get back to Sally and see how she was.

*   *   *

I let myself in the front door of the cottage and called

172

up the stairs.

'Sally. Sally. Are you all right?'

'Yes Helen I'm quite all right. You come and see.' She'd never called me Helen before. Perhaps we could be a comfort to one another.

'Helen you must come and see. Don't bother to take your coat off. Come at once.'

I tapped lightly on the bedroom door and walked in. Sally was sitting up in bed, her face wreathed in smiles, and kneeling beside her with his head on her lap was Richard. He looked up as I entered.

'Richard! You didn't go. What happened?'

'I mutinied,' he explained. 'I decided I couldn't leave Sally so I mutinied and refused to go.'

'What will they do to you?'

'They won't do anything. I don't think they minded.'

It seemed incredible to me. 'But after the training and preparation. They must have been as mad as anything. What happened exactly?'

'Oh Helen it was terrible. I was torn apart. I couldn't bear to let my friends down, to be separated from all the others, but I couldn't bear to be parted from Sally either.'

'What about the aversion treatment?'

'It didn't work. I didn't let it work. I just shut my mind when they switched the machine on.'

Sally smiled a little smugly, happy to know that Richard's feelings had been too strong for the mind machine.

'What did Dr Franks say when you told him?' I asked.

'He took it very calmly. He said that since the aversion treatment hadn't worked I shouldn't be able to go. They couldn't risk having a rogue male on board.'

'No of course they couldn't. A rogue male.' I laughed hysterically at the realization that Sally and Richard were together again and that they would be staying on the Earth. They might not stay at Bannockside, they might move somewhere else, but what did it matter? It didn't matter if they went to America or Australia as long as they didn't go on that one-way trip to Eden.

'I can't tell you how happy I am that you're not going.'

I could see that Sally and Richard were delirious at being together again, but was there still some slight flaw in their happiness?

'What's the matter? Everything's all right, isn't it?'

They both looked at me very seriously. Sally spoke. 'Please try to understand, dear Helen. To go to Eden was our destiny. We were born for it, and trained for it, and now the others have all gone and we are left behind, separated from them.'

'You'll be able to settle down doing something else,' I said, 'won't you?'

They shook their heads sadly, first Sally then Richard, and my joy at knowing they hadn't gone turned to ashes at the bitterness of their disappointment. I wished that they could have gone.

'We shall have to wait another year now,' said Sally.

'A year? What do you mean?'

'Dr Franks has arranged for us to go on the French rocket in 2006,' Richard explained.

I stood there open-mouthed, baffled, confused, my happiness at having them still with me shattered once more.

'There are five ships being used for the Eden expedition, two from America and three from Europe. The French is the third to leave.'

Sally reached out to take my hand. 'Please don't begrudge us our rightful destiny, Helen. Please try to understand. We have to go. We want to go. It will be nearly thirty years before we are reunited with the others, but we shall see them again, so please be happy for us, Helen.'

What could I say?

'We'll send you a card every Christmas.'

'How can you?' I wept. 'Please don't make fun of me Richard.'

'It's true Helen. Only a radiocard of course. When we're six months out the message will take three months to get back but it'll reach you. When we reach Eden we shall

174

send a message to say what it's like, but that'll take fifteen years to get back.'

'I shall be dead by then.'

'We shall always remember you and think of you and love you, Helen. You must always remember us, remember your distant relations on another world.'

'I'm going to the Memory Deletion tomorrow.'

'No you're not. You're not going to forget us, you're going to remember us always and be happy for us and proud of our exciting adventures.'

'I shall have nothing to live for. I shall be no use to anybody.'

'There's somebody who needs you very much,' said Sally quietly, 'and he's had to manage without you for nearly twenty years, but he's never given up waiting, has he?'

'You mean George,' I whispered. 'He's never asked me to join him.'

'Because he knew you wouldn't leave us, but soon you'll be free to love George.'

'I don't know,' I said. 'It's been so long. We might not get on now.'

'I know you will,' Sally assured me. 'I've known Mr Bradwell longer than you have, Mrs Bradwell, because I was in front of you in the queue at the vet's. Remember my poor tortoise? I thought the vet was very kind and very handsome. I could have fallen for him myself if he hadn't been too old and if I hadn't already got my eye on Richard.'

'Ring him up now,' Richard insisted. 'Here's the number, on his last card. I'll dial it for you.'

A circle of light appeared on the visiphone screen as Richard began dialling, and after a few seconds it gave way to the image of a familiar face, older and thinner than when I had seen it before, but still with the same kind eyes, the same patient smile.

'Why Helen. I can't tell you how wonderful it is to see you after all these years.'